WHAT YOU MIGHT FIND

SPINELESS WONDERS
PO Box 220, Strawberry Hills
New South Wales, Australia, 2012
www.shortaustralianstories.com.au

First published by Spineless Wonders 2018

Typeset in Adobe Garamond Pro
Printed and bound by Lightning Source Australia

National Library of Australia Cataloguing-in-Publication entry
What You Might Find /Richard Holt
1st ed.
978-1-925052-36-7 (pbk)
A823.4

This project has been assisted by the Australian Government through the Australia Council, its arts funding and advisory body.

RICHARD HOLT is a writer from Melbourne. His microfiction has been published by Spineless Wonders and by UK publisher Gumbo Press. His short stories have been published in *Visible Ink*, *Etchings*, *Cuttlefish*, *Victorian Writer*, *Best Australian Sports Writing* (Random House, 1997) and online in the *Irish Literary Review*. He was a semi-finalist in the Raymond Carver Short Story Competition, 2016, and is a past winner of the Antipodes Sorrento Short Story Competition. His poetry is included in *Australian Love Poems* (Inkerman & Blunt, 2013) and has been broadcast on Radio National and 3RRR. His non-fiction writing has appeared in journals including *ArtLink*, *World Art*, *Art Monthly* and AR (*The Architectural Review*) and his creative non-fiction has appeared in a number of collections of sports writing. He also produces text-based videos, artworks and interactive text-based installations for public spaces, and was co-founder of Melbourne zine store Sticky. He is a former recipient of a Maurice Saxby Mentorship for Children's Writers and Illustrators and was Bayside Writer in Residence in 2013.

What you might find

RICHARD HOLT

CONTENTS

'Ind
125mn
375220
$

Afloat

My uncle arrived at a distant archipelago on a raft he'd made from flooring offcuts and bamboo poles from Bunnings. He stumbled into a resort reception area asking – please – if they had anything for sunburn … only he didn't have any money on account of his wallet getting washed overboard during the storm.

The storm went through two days ago, said the clerk.

That long? said my uncle.

Where'd you come from? The clerk tugged the collar of his Hawaiian shirt.

Liesterfield.

On the mainland! That's a hundred kilometres! Does anyone know you're here?

My uncle looked at him, a little perplexed. Well … yes, he said. You do.

That's about when he collapsed. He came to in a luxury suite. For a few weeks, before hitching a ride home on a trawler, he was the toast of the island.

When my uncle died the people of Liesterfield, a place of neatly trimmed lawns, where politeness is valued above all things, soon forgot him.

But elsewhere my uncle's story is joyfully retold. And the people who love to hear it live in a place off the coast where the water is warm and clear, the sun shines on palm-fringed beaches and nobody hurries.

Fading towards infinity

Helga's counting stitches.

What percent of nothing is nothing? says Lester.

What? she says. What are you talking about?

Nothing.

As usual, she says.

What percent, then? he says. Could be none. Could be a hundred. How's that work?

What's it matter? says Helga.

It matters, says Lester.

~

Helga looks at him with his scraps of paper and his scrawls and his hair gone white and Einstein-crazy. He's shuffling and scribbling and sometimes looking thoughtfully at the ceiling, which fools no one 'cos she's the only one in the room to fool and why he even thinks she'd be looking at him she doesn't know.

He's got theories. That's his problem. Theories about everything.

I've got no time for your theories, Lester, she says.

He looks up. Licks a corner of his top lip. You oughtta, he says.

~

The Labrador is lazy and deaf. She slouches between them turning her head like she's watching tennis, same as she used to when she could still hear them talking. She's turning one way and the other and the bucket contraption on her head that's stopping her licking herself half to death goes scrape, scrape, scrape on the floorboards.

Christ, says Helga. When's she back at the vet?

What? says Lester.

The vet, she says. When's she back?

The dog sneezes.

Seventeenth, says Lester.

Helga puts down her magazine. She plonks it hard onto the coffee table.

What? says Lester.

What's today? says Helga.

Monday.

Helga waits, brow scrunched like a cat at a mouse hole. The dog, as if it ought to contribute, chooses the moment for a puffy fart. She farts a lot these days. The clock tick-tick-ticks. The bucket scrapes the boards. His turn, her turn…

Twentieth.

Right. And?

What?

The dog?

The vet just got back; she's seeing her on the twenty-fourth, says Lester. Friday.

What? says Helga. She picks up her magazine again, rolls it and wrings it tight.

I've got a theory, says Lester.

~

Lester says nought and infinity are the same thing.

How'd you figure that? says Joe.

Lester explains. It's dimensional, he says. See the flag: how far's it away?

Two hundred and nine, says Joe. What are you using?

Driver, says Lester. But I can touch it. In this dimension. He waves his 2-wood up and down. See in this dimension it's nothing. Right there. I call it dimensional relativity.

You sure about that?

What? says Lester.

Driver? says Joe. With a tail wind?

Three-iron then? says Lester.

Joe turns his club so Lester can read the number on the head, then he smiles. You might be onto somethin' there, Lester, says Joe.

About the 3-iron? says Lester.

Infinity, says Joe. You gonna, I dunno, tell someone? They use stuff like that in rockets and things, you know.

Nah, says Lester. Infinity, he says, as he takes his stance, with a glance towards the green. He's got a sort of a twitch at the start of his swing. He doesn't know why. He's always had it.

Two hundred and nine, says Joe, at the top of Lester's backswing.

Lester's drive goes about 120 into the right-hand rough.

~

Helga's stopped caring about me, says Lester.

What? says Joe. Helga?

It's as if I'm not there.

Nah.

It's true. Lester swipes at a hovering bee.

You sure? says Joe.

I reckon.

D'you still love her?

Sure I do. Why d'you think I married her? She's everything.

How long've you been married? says Joe.

~

Things change, says Joe.

~

Playin' Friday? says Joe.

Can't, says Lester. Dog's getting its bucket off.

Why doesn't Helga take it? says Joe.

Lester watches a mother duck and her brood plop, one by one, into the lake behind the eighteenth green. He says, She wants me to do it. She's got something on. One of her groups.

How many groups she got? says Joe.

I dunno, says Lester. Lots. Groups for ev'rything from what I can tell.

See, that's the thing, says Joe.

Look at them ducks, says Lester. Happy as Larry.

You okay, Lester? says Joe.

~

Lester puts the telly on. There's a nature show on cable. African grasslands right there in front of him. The wildebeests are taking a beating. He's got his notebooks out. His pens and pencils in a row. He's thinking but it's as if he's thinking mud. He's waiting for microwaved leftovers to cool. There's a note from Helga but he hasn't bothered reading it. When there's a note on his dinner in the fridge he knows what it'll say. So he hasn't even unfolded it. Don't wait up. Plus there'll most likely be a list of things to do. Things he doesn't need to know, like a load of whites that needs hanging. The lions are closing in on a calf with a gammy leg.

The dog lolls at Lester's feet. Since the bucket came off she's been kind of quiet, like she misses it, somehow.

The little wildebeest goes down.

~

D'you reckon there's a fifth dimension? says Lester.

Sure, says Joe. It's over in the rough along the twelfth fairway.

Yeah. I suppose. How many balls d'you reckon you've lost in there?

Down the years? Plenty, says Joe. They've got one of them black holes along there.

Lester laughs.

How's it with Helga? says Joe.

Same, says Lester. How would I know? She's hardly home any more.

You tried flowers on her? says Joe.

She'd only laugh.

Really?

I reckon. What are you using?

Four-iron, says Lester.

Too much club, says Joe.

I've got a theory, says Lester.

~

When he gets around to reading the note it says she's away for the night. There's nothing about maybe calling. Nothing about missing anything or being lonely without … or can't wait … like she used to say all the time even if she wasn't going anywhere really – even if they'd be seeing each other later that evening. Nothing about him at all. Maybe his trouble is he remembers it all. Because whatever's up with the outings and the not saying those things to him anymore, she seems happy. What's past is past for her. She's got her groups now. She's got her activities. She doesn't need the memories the way he does. He's watching something about clouds. Fascinating things clouds. He's thinking about water everywhere. His pencils are still in the drawer in the spare room. They need sharpening. His notebooks are all closed in a stack on the table beside him. He's drifting like translucent cirrus.

Helga says, I left a message on the machine.

I never use the machine, he says. The messages are always for you, anyway.

She says, It was only one extra night.

Lester says, You ought to have been here. The dog had a turn. You ought to maybe have at least tried more than once. What's that damn mobile for then, anyway? he says.

The battery was flat, says Helga. I didn't take the charger. I didn't know I'd need it. It was only one extra night. I left a message, says Helga.

The dog is doing the tennis thing again – head one way and then the other.

Was it good then? says Lester.

Was what good, Lester? says Helga. Do you even know what I was doing?

The winery tour, says Lester. He wouldn't have known if she hadn't written it on the calendar in the kitchen. But he doesn't tell her that. Was it good? he says.

It was good, says Helga. Interesting.

Lester remembers suggesting they take a drive up that way. That was back when things weren't quite so … stale … is that it? So treacherous. He remembers her laughing. What's a teetotaller like you want with wineries, Lester? she said.

Tell me about it, says Lester.

Christ Lester, she says. I'm tired. Can't it wait?

I got a theory for you, Lester, says Joe.

Really? says Lester.

Yeah, says Joe. A brunette. Friend of my sisters.

No. I'm okay, says Lester. Really. We're okay.

Positive? says Joe. I can … you know … introduce you.

Not much of a theory, says Lester.

I guess. Well if you ever—

I've got a theory for you, Joe, says Lester.

What's that? says Joe.

Infinity, says Lester.

Here we go, says Joe, stooping to tee up.

The time it'll take for every drop of water that's ever been to go, at some time, from the deepest part of the ocean to the outer reaches of the atmosphere – that's infinity.

Blimey. Really? I thought it was like forever, says Joe.

It is, says Lester. But it's something concrete too. It has to be. It's a number. It's a time. It's nothing and something. And everything and more. Think about water going around. Think about it.

You thinkin' about going round the water?

Eh?

That damn hazard, says Joe. If I lose another ball in there I'm gonna—

You oughtta lay up. Pitch over it, says Lester. You can't drive it anymore. Not since you hurt your back.

I can drive it, says Joe. I just gotta hit it sweet.

Where's that water been? says Lester. It's been all round the world. It's as old as the planet; come down through the ages. Constant cycles. It's been inside dinosaurs for all we know. It's been down in the ocean. And it's been up in the clouds.

An' now it's spread out across the fourth fairway. Waiting. Should have stayed in them dinosaurs, I reckon.

~

There's not even a note. Just dinner on a plate in the fridge and a bill that needs paying laid out on the bench so he can't miss it, with highlighter over the due-by, five days ago.

He thinks maybe waves are the answer. Waves and currents. Because there must be an answer, he reckons. There must be a way. The world's so full of energy. All over.

Helga used to call him a-bit-old-to-be-a-greenie sometimes when he'd tell her ideas like that. She'd say, they'll work something out, Lester, besides…

Lester gets a pencil out. Sharpens it as pointy as a pin. He starts to scribble. Pretty soon he's got papers scattered everywhere. He's thinking about permanence and impermanence. He's got another theory on the way.

Five days and nights have come and gone. Just him and the dog. No notes. He's checked the machine every night. Nothing.

~

The Constable asks if he can have a word.

Sure, says Lester. Come in. Come in.

Lester wishes he'd had the chance to tidy. What with Helga still not back he's let the place go a bit.

Take a seat, says Lester.

The Constable declines. He says, there's been an accident. I'm terribly sorry, he says.

Lester descends slowly onto the arm of the couch. An accident?

~

After taking the dog for a walk Lester thinks about Helga years ago, slunk down beside him on her mother's couch, her arms around his neck, her breath sparkling bright, her wet kisses, her desire like a charged evening sky when there's dry lightning on the horizon and a storm brewing.

~

Where you been? says Joe.

Things to do, says Lester.

You okay?

Sure, says Lester. Been working on something, he says.

Must be another theory, says Joe. Can't have been your swing. You're still hitting it left to right. You're getting ahead of the ball.

Yeah, I know, says Lester. Some things are beyond fixing.

Anything you need to talk about? says Joe. You heard from Helga?

Nup.

Lester?

Things change, says Lester. I guess. Gotta get used to it. Just me and the dog.

So it's over? says Joe.

Things change. Like you said. It's all good. What are you using? says Lester.

Seven-iron, says Joe. You?

Driver maybe.

Driver?

Tee it up high. Send it into orbit, says Lester.

On a par 3? says Joe.

So it goes on forever, says Lester. Like that astronaut that time.

You're crazy, says Joe.

Maybe, says Lester. Just a theory.

Go the 7-iron, Lester, says Joe.

Yeah, says Lester. I suppose. He lingers over his bag. The weight of the driver is sweet in his gloved hand.

Red line

They've been complaining on the radio about the Red Line doors again. Always complaining, says Rosa. Some people are always complaining.

I dunno, says Daryl, those doors close too quick.

You gotta be alert, she says. People these days. With their headphones and their texting. No one pays attention.

The escalator jags as it rattles them down. The air smells of hot brake pads, burnt oil and sweat – the subway in summer.

On the platform a group of boys sings doo-wop for small change. They've got a crowd. Daryl slows to listen. It's not the sort of music you hear every day. Layers as luscious as cream cake. He could have sung like that if he'd had the chance.

Stop dawdling, says Rosa. She marches along the platform, heading for where the last carriage stops so she'll be close to the exit when they get out at Market, where Liz and Harrison have their apartment. Rosa likes to think ahead.

Daryl catches the harmonies.

Rosa says, late again. She gestures towards an overhanging screen. She's not patient with things anymore. She's dogged, that's what he'd call it. And when she's riled up, like now, she gets that intent, slightly put-out look. Daryl remembers it from when he used to fuss over her, hoping she'd want to be his girl. She doesn't like fuss anymore. Not unless she's making it.

Relax, says Daryl. There's no hurry.

I don't want to relax, says Rosa. Relaxing is for twenty-year-olds with time on their hands. I'm fifty-four, Daryl. Things ought to work properly by now.

Just for you, I suppose. TransNet probably couldn't care.

Well, they ought to, says Rosa.

Nice singing, says Daryl.

Doesn't help the trains run on time?

Makes the waiting better.

Bah.

Daryl loves her seriousness. It reminds him how she used to be about all the causes she had. The environment. Animal rights. Justice for this and that. He gets it into his head that he'd actually like to hug her right on the platform. He imagines the consequences. Take her in his arms. He'd rock her back and kiss her, maybe. Conspire with gravity to get the upper hand for once.

Daryl can't hide a grin.

What?

What, what? he says.

You're looking goofy, says Rosa.

Really? Am I?

Yeah. Are you feeling alright? she says. Are you after something?

The doo-wop boys are doing Elvis. Trains clatter in and out on other lines. Expresses shake the platforms as they pass.

I ought to get lessons, says Daryl.

What?

Singing. I've got a good enough voice.

Yeah, says Rosa. For mime.

When the Red Line train finally arrives it's as if everybody's forgotten what they're waiting for. There's no announcement and the screens say there's no train, but there it is. People the length of the platform mutter to each other – is this the Red Line uptown? No one's one hundred percent sure but they scramble to get on anyway.

Rosa calls out, Come on, Daryl.

Daryl's been watching a family – five of them, each with their own tub of nuggets. Maybe they won some sort of prize, thinks Daryl, slotting in behind them and edging towards the train. All you can eat. A year's supply. Something like that.

He pushes forward. At the edge of the platform he smells hot brake pads and cooking fat. The boy in front clambers on board. A space opens and he steps through the doors, glancing across, expecting Rosa beside him.

She's not there. He turns around. Sees her stooping to pick up her ticket from the concrete platform. Why doesn't she keep it in her purse? It's one of the new plastic ones, loaded with credit. Most people hate them. They want the old paper ones back. Rosa says people who think like that are disorganised. She fumbles, trying to pick it up.

Clutching it at last, she lurches for the carriage. The Red Line train doors close, perfectly in sync. They slice across with the certainty of guillotines.

Daryl's jaw slackens. He mouths bye through the glass as the train moves off. He wonders if he should blow a kiss, but before he can she's out of view.

The doo-wop boys start a new tune for the disembarked passengers scurrying towards the up escalator. Rosa looks around at the platform emptying.

The boys stop mid-song. No one's watching.

At that moment Rosa believes in fate. Or maybe waiting for the next Red Line train's just not worth the effort. She can call Liz and Harrison any time. So she turns and walks out past the singers gathering their coins, transformed, by their silence into a motley slack of teenagers.

Rosa steps aboard the escalator. It clunks and rattles her upwards towards an expanding chink of grey-blue winter sky.

The temptation
of Ludovico Carracci

Radiance, says the guide, adjusting her spectacles.

It's her first day. This internship feels like the beginning of everything she's ever wanted.

Her listeners, gathered in front of a massive canvas, nod agreement. At the back, a couple who are tagging along mock her enthusiasm with shared, wide-eyed glances.

The guide sweeps her hand in an arc that takes in the whole of the image before her. Of all the artist's works, she says, it is this one piece that captures the spiritual moment most precisely. The ascension. Here we see Ludovico at the height of his powers. Notice how the virgin is drawn upwards, made weightless by the light from above.

~

Portia returns just as the bread is coming out of the oven to make way for the roasting meat. She slaps her brother's back. Giancarlo, she says. How do the peasants fare this morning?

Hard working, he says. Unlike some. Father went looking for you. They said, in town, you'd been up near the artists' place again.

Near. No, not near. In. And why not? The painters are good enough for Father Antonio to want their pictures in his church. Good enough that the town should brag about them — that they're here in Bologna, not in Florence or Rome. Not in Venice.

But they're not so good as I should be allowed to visit them, eh, Brother?

True. Little good anywhere you choose to go, says Giancarlo. Artists indeed. And your mother at her wit's end. And your dear Nona cursing you in her sleep.

Of course – she would – the woman's mad.

She makes sense, at least, to worry for your soul.

Sense! She's as mad as a cat. Mad and old. Dried and shrivelled like a fallen leaf.

Tch.

Portia sweeps him aside.

In the big room where the family dine their father is cleaning the kitchen knives. Sharpening them on a stone. He lifts one eyelid as she enters. Daughter, he says, in a voice that admonishes and admires in equal measure.

She drapes herself around his bent neck, thick black hair as untamed as hawthorn. He smells her earthy breath. There is wine on it already. When she kisses his cheek he cannot help but smile, for she is as wild as he once thought himself.

Sharpest of the knives is the one he uses to carve the meat. A kid has been slaughtered to mark the visit of the eldest daughter, Donna, whose marriage to a second cousin of the Duke has enhanced the family's reputation. In Bologna reputations are not easily made. Everyone is considered a bumpkin who has no claim to nobility. Papa separates the rare meat from the bone. Blood-red juices glisten at the cut.

Donna arranges herself at the table. Her maidservant is eating in the kitchen. In the yard, with the chickens, her boy minds the horses on which they arrived; he is watched, in turn, by the neighbours, who are filled with jealous veneration of the elder daughter's new status.

So, Sister – Donna pats her mouth with the corner of a napkin. How do you fare for suitors in my absence?

Giancarlo snickers. The others focus on their plates.

Your absence is the least of my concerns, says Portia. Suffice that fewer dull, rich eunuchs trouble us since you left. I owe you that much.

Portia! Papa forgets the knife in his hand. Its point draws circles as he demands, at least, the act of decorum.

Nona pipes up from her chair in the corner – says she knew a young man once.

Fascinating, says Portia. Taking her plate she excuses herself. She slams the door on the bickering in her wake, leaving like a fire-starter bored by the flames of her crime.

Outside in the Tuscan glow she seeks out the horse-boy. Finds him brushing down a bay mare. When the boy ignores her she sidles close, leans in and whispers to his reddening ear. You could run your brush through my hair. Rub me down. Prepare me to ride. I'd be a fine mount for a healthy lad. She reaches for hay, allowing the boy a glimpse full down her loose-tied bodice. Sensing the eyes on them both through the windows all around, she cups her hand and pushes it against his crutch. How does my sister reward you when you please her? What does she give you?

He squirms. Nothing, he says. She lets me inside to warm by her fire.

I'd have you inside too. She squeezes. My fire is hotter. Hers – bah! As cold as last month's ashes.

My mistress is a good woman. I'll not hear—

You'll not hear much from her worth hearing is my guess. Perhaps a bit of frigid moaning – and that only if she lets you share her bed? Does she have you sleep with her?

My lady! Please.

I knew she was stupid. If I had a boy like you to myself I'd have made a man of you by now. Saddle me a horse.

Pardon?

The grey.

Your sister's favourite?

Perfect.

The studio occupies an abandoned blacksmith's compound. A forge heats the central square. Overlooking it are the balconies of a series of villas. Turned to face inward, like pigs around a trough, the rough stone and brick buildings house the pupils and apprentices. Some of the rooms are used for mixing paints and preparing canvases and panels. In others the pictures that have made the studio famous are emerging. Cartoons in black or red chalk, underpainted scenes and a few grand canvases awaiting varnishing before they can be delivered to the churches and patrons who have commissioned them.

Apart from a few portraits the panels are either biblical or interpretations of classical stories. So it is that piety and abandon vie for the attention of anyone who enters the academy of the Carracci.

The place buzzes with activity. Artists at the easels or preparing materials. There are pockets of loud conversation. A woman in one of the upstairs rooms is singing.

At the centre of it all is Ludovico. He is the eldest – the master. He leans across a table over which are strewn drawings for a new commission, a cycle of classical frescoes.

Portia is not the only woman. A wealthy matron is talking to Annibale, Ludovico's younger cousin. The boy is prodigiously talented and almost equally wicked. Scattered around the compound are other local women who, like Portia, seem to have no great purpose here. Sometimes the artists call on them to pose for students, to fetch wine, to provide a critical opinion: Girl, how do you find this angel?

The loveliest of the women is Mariarosa. In spite of her aloofness it is she to whom the artists pay most attention. Agostino, Annibale's brother, has her posing, draped in velvet. Her hair is rust red. Her eyes are a particular green he mixes from pigments crushed from beetle wings and semi-precious stones. She acknowledges Portia with the smallest nod. It is all that is needed to fire her hot dart of jealousy.

Portia's curse is silent. Her smile betrays nothing. She turns and makes a bee-line for Ludovico.

Bella Portia, he says, looking up. I thought you were needed at your father's house – your sister's visit?

I have had enough of her already, she says. We don't get on. I haven't the stomach for her small talk or her fine manners. What are you working on?

Ludovico shows her a rough sketch. *The Temptation of St Anthony.* I'm looking for a virgin for it.

Not here you're not, she says.

Perhaps Mariarosa?

Ah. The pretty harlot?

She has the face for it. Innocence and rapture.

Innocence! Who's it for, anyway – this *Temptation*?

A merchant from Milan. He wishes to donate it to the basilica – down-payment on an eternal life.

A large piece then?

Like most rich men his earthly days have not been altogether saintly. He needs something substantial.

Portia does not respond. Her thoughts, instead, have been accosted by the possibilities. The basilica. Everyone in the town would see it … see her in the guise of the blessed virgin. If she could divert the artist from that fish-faced strumpet, she could be the one. She deserves that much from Ludovico and his cousins. They have been liberal enough with her muse.

Do you like it?

Of course. You make so much from a few quick lines. But you can't be serious about the virgin. You know I pose better than she does – always feeling faint – Oh, Ludovico. Oh, Annibale … a moment to compose – such feigned frailty.

Perhaps it's the frailty that makes her well suited.

Portia puts an arm around the artist's shoulders. Though he is the oldest he is in good shape. She has thought of him as fatherly, preferring his cousin, when he can be distracted from the redhead's attentions. But Portia is no stranger to pragmatism.

She can rearrange her feelings in the service of greater purpose, and, though the thought is fresh, she doubts if she ever felt so purposeful. She whispers, I could make you change your mind.

I dare say, he says. I am not committed to the other girl, though she insists it should be her. Perhaps your chance to convince me will come.

Perhaps, says Portia. I will be in the kitchens if you need me. She leaves with a parting kiss as light on his cheek as a squirrel-hair brush.

When her sister's horse-boy arrives Portia is draped on the wide sill of an upstairs window. Warm breeze swirls in the artists' quadrangle. She watches the breathless page as he scans the yard for her. The knowledge that he has come all the way from her father's house to find her provokes the slightest smile. Turning her head, she sees the lad through the window, casting about for any sign of her or the horse (which she has lent to Annibale so he can visit a cloth merchant who has new stock of good canvas).

The boy scans the upper windows. She ducks back into the shadows but continues to watch.

Portia! Ludovico's deep voice makes her start.

Come to your senses about the blessed Mary?

No need to be contemptuous. I have considered it. I thought I might see how well you do. Would you like to come downstairs?

Portia does not wish to reveal herself so soon to her sister's boy. Draw me up here, she says. With the light behind.

It's not … then again, says the artist … yes … why not?

After retrieving a drawing board, paper and charcoal from another room, Ludovico sets the pose. Portia arches towards the window light. He has her raise her hands, with palms towards her, fingers stretched taut in front of her breasts. They emphasise her ample curves. Ludovico has her look to the heavens. You should appear breathless, he says, mouth open, but only just.

She pushes her tongue against opened teeth.

Perfect.

Is that your idea of innocence? she says.

The basilica padres are not as bloodless as you might think. I've learnt I do well to please desires to which they will not admit. Let the godly women call such expressions ecstasy. The men, in their reverent reflection, will make of them what they will.

I might make a better virgin than I imagined, says Portia.

Indeed.

What of Mariarosa?

I may choose to sketch her as well.

A contest?

Why not?

Just draw, snorts Portia, leaning back. From the corner of her eye she spies, in the yard below, the boy sitting slump-shouldered on the edge of a trough.

The sun is setting behind her by the time Ludovico finishes his study. It is some hours since Annibale returned, tormenting the boy with his insistence that the horse belonged to him. Now the boy has taken the grey mare and fled. Most of the loitering women have returned to the disapproving safety of their families. The apprentices are cleaning brushes and sweeping the yard.

Mariarosa has been hovering in the upstairs halls and rooms. Keeping an eye on her virgin rival. On the artist. Agitation has cast a stain on her wan complexion that the dimming light cannot hide.

The drawing, when Ludovico finishes it, is as fine as any he has made. Portia does not need his exclamation to know it. The light that frames her heightens the effect – of glorious beauty and saintliness. And, yes, something beyond that. Ecstasy. She watches greedily as the artist considers his work as if it were by another hand altogether. Another master.

The light on the sill is golden as she peels out of the window, bruises stiffening where the weight of the pose pressed so long on the stone.

Is there still a contest? she whispers to his ear.

No contest, he says. You are the one.

Ha. She shakes the soreness from her joints. Her hair settles over her shoulders.

The artist offers her wine and fruit. Portia drinks to the moment the painting is revealed to the town. She drinks to what they will say about her then. And to the consternation this will cause her rival.

When Ludovico offers to find a carriage to take her home she declines, delicately accepting his next offer, but only after eliciting his assurance again.

There is no question now, my sweet, he says. Ahh, I feel young to have drawn such a thing. And it was you. All along it was you.

Mariarosa does not appear at the studio the next morning. After a week word arrives that she has left Bologna for Milan. Ludovico forgets about her. He no longer wants her pretty compliments. Since the afternoon he drew Portia by the window, he feels, more than ever, the master of his art. His virgin-model satisfies whatever desires he has. Her affection for him is no longer affected. In every way she longs to be with him – to watch him paint. To talk with him and lie with him, excited both by the basilica painting with her image at its apex and by the man who has drafted it so perfectly. It progresses well. Her beatific face framed by the light of heaven. In a few weeks he will present it to the merchant who will be visiting from Milan. The merchant will present it to the church fathers as the centrepiece of their new basilica. In so doing the unlikeable man will claim, by its glory, his piece of eternal life. By this painting, too, the artist's reputation will be sealed, perhaps even beyond the few years he has left of his craft. Beyond his mortal time. And Portia will gain, in her turn, the awed respect of those townsfolk who have so long dismissed her. And she will have whatever portion of eternity is due such a painting as this.

~

The guide takes a moment to reflect. There's a new mystery surrounding this picture, she says. During its recent conservation, X-rays revealed the overpainted face of another model – a brunette – beneath the red-headed virgin we know today.

Also discovered, beneath the bracing of the canvas, was an inscription in the artist's hand.

The woman shifts a little uncomfortably, checking her notes for the correct translation.

For Bella Portia, the inscription reads. May she forgive me, in time, the moment I substituted her for that Milanese merchant's whore.

The swimmer

One morning, while running, Ollie Perovic thought he spotted a swimmer momentarily within the featurelessness of the new day's grey, but he couldn't be sure. There was no colour, no contrast. No light or dark. No horizon. Later he thought perhaps he heard a distant voice calling but, as it was early spring, plenty of boisterous groups were using the foreshore – boot camp warriors and football clubs – so he thought nothing of it. No one passed as he trudged up the hill to the beacon and over to the footbridge.

Only later that day, as he headed back to the office from Soup King, did Ollie recall the two possibilities, the swimmer and the voice, each as uncertain as each other. The coincidence of these memories brought about a kind of dread, which stuck with him all afternoon. He was unable to concentrate on the Pathways Report and found himself checking online news sites every few minutes. Though the media reported no one missing, his brooding uncetainty persisted.

A week later, as he shuffled along the sand of Eastern Beach in the thickness of another fog, he imagined he heard a call from the direction of the waves. With barely a thought he pulled off his running shoes and t-shirt and leapt into the water. He was a better swimmer than runner and had put three hundred metres between himself and the shore before he realised the icy conditions were getting the better of him. His limbs began to cramp. An all-over shiver ran through him. Looking to the shore he could just make out a figure on the beachside path, jogging in a heavy, plodding gait that seemed familiar. Ollie Perovic called, without hope, across the waves with all that was left of his flagging strength.

Her dark ground

Adelie kept a locked book of recipes for black. Thirty or so, each with its mood and purpose.

Every canvas she painted began as one of these shadowy combinations. Choosing the right one, mixing it, spreading it over white gesso, was all that kept her painting. And painting was all that kept her. Only when her chosen ground was as close to perfect as she could make it would she obliterate it beneath the effusive colour around which her reputation had been built.

Free market

This then was all that was left. Dex's climb had been stratospheric. At thirty he'd been ready to fly. Too close to the sun. The crash hit hard. The auditors did their job for once. His bosses held him to account for the same things they'd once demanded of him. Everything disintegrated. Now this was all. A torn mattress, a dirty blanket, a transistor radio and a bunch of clothes. Four walls and a barred window. He kicked his belongings together into a corner, sucked his last cigarette almost to the filter then flicked the glowing butt into the pile. Black latex smoke started curling upwards. It pooled beneath the ceiling. A lick of purple flame struck up among his t-shirts and jeans. He glanced at the door. Now at least he had options. Freedom of choice. That's what made this country great.

The perfect house

As soon as Leesa walked in she knew it was the place. 'It's perfect. A real house, not a lousy shack.'

The secluded location was ideal. There'd be no one to disturb them.

As they went from room to room – five in all, kitchen, bath, a small living area and a cosy bedroom – their excitement grew.

'Yeah,' said Cameron, who didn't generally say a lot, 'it's the one, alright.'

When they reached the bedroom Leesa wrapped him tight and waited for the spark in his eye. He dug his fingers into the back of her jeans and drew her up close.

'We've got everything we need,' he said. It was a half-question.

'Sure.' She handed him the wine bottle from her handbag, its gold liquid catching the light through the window. 'The sun's about to set. Come on. Let's go up on the hill to watch.'

They stepped into the crisp valley air outside. Cameron uncapped the bottle. He pulled a rag from his pocket and stuffed it tight into the neck. Within minutes they'd be on the rise opposite, enthralled by each other and by the beautiful crackle and spark and glow as the old timbers blazed in the night.

1975: Glam rockers on the prowl

I get my first view of the sun just as it's about to go down. Fitzroy Street in the daytime isn't the right place for the likes of us. Nighttime makes more sense around here. Baz and me and the boys. Baz'll have his platforms on. His spandex and his spangles. Baz'll get a sashay going – swing his arse like a pony. Swing it for the beer-slugging lads from the suburbs. They'll tell him that the strip joint is up the hill and he'll blow them a kiss. Poser. You could get yourself in plenty of trouble down here. Baz is trouble. But he can sing like a bird. Like an angel cast from heaven. He can take up wherever Ginger's guitar wants to take him. And the suburban boys'll be so pissed by the time we're finishing our set that it's them that'll be blowing him the kisses.

[from the Street Sweep Fitzroy St project]

The sifter

Something else I remember that's gone now is bets scrawled by hand by bookmakers' clerks. Their crayon swirls held everything a bookie needed to know – the race, the horse, the type of bet, the odds and the amount wagered. They were coded messages. Secrets.

My family weren't racing people. Instead I'd head across town during winter to watch football matches with my grandfather. On the way home my tram would stop outside the track.

~

The lining of his dirty gabardine coat bulges full of discarded hopes. I'm mesmerised. Though I'm just a boy I can tell this man's connection to the world the other passengers share has withered until it's barely a thread. He ignores everyone including the conductor. Everyone ignores him. In the bubble of his pungent self-possession he spreads across the space that spreads around him. Then the tickets emerge in clumps from the depths of his coat. He processes them like a machine. In his crumpled head he might retain little of his past. But he remembers every result from every race at the track today. Tote tickets and bookie stubs fall around him like dirty snow. The conductor scowls, but maintains his distance. No one watches but me. He sees me staring his way. His grin, toothless and vacant, is fleeting. He pulls another clump of tickets from his coat, lingering on one that looks as if it's been picked from the mud. He holds it to the light, smiles, then pushes it into the side of his shoe. I figure he deserves it. All that work collecting and sifting.

It never occurs to me that this might be a show of victory for my sake alone. But just a show nevertheless. Even a secret-sifter, I realise now, might feel the need to prove the worth of what he does.

Oblong

I was destined to write. It was Beggs who saw it first – 7D. Ah, Thompson, he said. Always the wordsmith. Yes, Sir, I said – not my finest line but the pressure was on. Perhaps, as you enjoy writing so much, I might set you a task … what do you say? Yes, Sir, I said. I must say I'm impressed, he said. It's not every day one is offered such an opportunity – a chance to create something lasting. Many might have resorted to the visual. But you've captured the very essence in written language. Bard-like … brilliant. Do you think? I said, warming to his response. I do, he said. He took another look at my creation. Yes, certainly. Incredible. Come with me, he said. Leading me by the earlobe he trudged me back to the classroom, muttering, all the while, extraordinary … quite extraordinary. Beggs showed me the possibilities. I had only dabbled. He opened my eyes. The whole board, Sir? Yes, Thompson, the whole board. Did he think the challenge would defeat me? Instead I found in it the true potential of the form. Concrete poetry – the board a solid block of letters. I will not write penis in the new footpath. I will not write penis in the new footpath. Over and over. I will not write penis. I will not write penis. The meter precise. The rhythm like heartbeats. I will not... I will not ... I will not...

The locked half-blood

Sometimes the only clue that the tide has turned is the sound of the slap of water on weathered timbers. Long after dark there's a pause, then the flow returns, but in the opposite direction. With a bit of luck the fish go on the bite.

With a bit of luck... Sometimes you wait what seems forever but the change never comes.

Catching anything? The thin voice is close, like a circling mosquito – almost ghostly. Whoever it belongs to must have crept up on Frank, quieter than the night. He takes a swig of water before turning. Being alone is harder than it ought to be. Not much, he says. He nods towards a bucket. His head-torch casts dim, bluish light into the slurry. A pair of flathead lie submerged, Yin and Yang, on their plastic circle of white.

Better than nothing.

S'pose so, says Frank. You trying your luck?

Tonight? says the stranger. Nah.

When Frank looks up, his torch captures a face he feels he knows. Not haven't-we-met kind of knows, but he recognises something in the eyes staring back – a straining tendril between hope and despair. And he 'gets' that this guy would turn up out of the blue, in the middle of nowhere. Not everyone could do it – it takes a certain kind of lonely. The newcomer is waiting for something, but he doesn't know what it is or where he will find it. Maybe he thinks a stranger fishing in the dark will be able to tell him.

Or maybe Frank's reading too much into the disengaged stare – might just be the deadening glow of the LEDs casting a pall on the stranger's complexion

Name's Frank, he says. You wanna pull up a pew?

The visitor – young fella, thirty maybe – looks perplexed. Tilts his head. His shrug has a shiver within it. He says nothing.

Frank picks up his catch and tosses it into the dark. The flatheads re-enter their own world with two distinct splashes. It's their lucky day, he says, upending the bucket to make a stool like his own.

Rhys, says the stranger, taking a seat. Clouds separate to the east.

Frank isn't sure he heard right. Rhys, was it? He offers a moonlit handshake. So if you're not fishing…

Might throw a line in tomorrow.

Tomorrow, says Frank. Bit of a cold front coming. Don't leave it too late. He swigs water from a Coke bottle. Offers it to the newcomer, who declines. Not many know this spot, says Frank. You come here much?

Came up once with me dad, says Rhys. For a whole week. We never saw anyone. It was just him and me. Wouldn't happen these days.

Planet's getting too crowded, says Frank.

Rhys shrugs. Gotta roll with the punches.

~

You spend enough time talking to people about yourself – professional people trying to help – eventually you get to thinking. You get to know how the talking stuff works and to knowing it's not necessarily the words that matter but the talking and the listening and the spaces in between.

After you've been talking to people that way for a while, strangers mostly – seems like half your life – you start thinking, there's two of us doing this. After we're done I reckon we both feel better about ourselves. Main difference is one of us gets paid to do it. Eventually you get the idea, maybe you ought to get paid for talking to people too. Talk about their problems for a change. You could do it with your eyes closed.

You get to thinking it so much you do something about it. You become what you thought you'd never be. School wasn't ever really your thing. You sign up for a diploma course. When you mention it your counsellor says, yeah, sure, it's a great idea. But you know her well enough to know she doesn't think you have it in you. Even with your best interests at heart she can't help thinking it's just something else for you to bugger up.

Frank wishes his train had been on time. Most of the chairs in the tute room are taken. New students sizing each other up. He squeezes past a group looking at something on a girl's phone. They're just kids, fresh faced, yearning to learn, desperate to go forth and help the less fortunate. By the looks they've suffered little more than the odd, garden-variety tragedy between them. Not that Frank thinks this uncharitably. He tries not to judge. But observations … well, it's a free country. They're happy enough. Good luck to them.

There's a couple of older guys in suits. He has no idea why they're here. A nervy beatnik-looking hipster keeps his head low. Nearby, a woman in a tailored jacket has her textbooks and pens carefully arranged in front of her. At the far end of the room there's a woman about his own age – old-enough-to-know-better, he calls it – who catches his eye. She indicates the vacant seat next to hers.

My name's Maureen, she says. People mostly call me Mo.

Frank, he says. People have called me a lot of things.

Nice things, I hope.

People are people, he says.

That's why I'm here, says Mo. What about yourself?

Same, I guess. Morbid fascination. Something to do.

I've been trying to sus this mob out, says Mo. That lot are a bit of a worry. The prefects, she says, with a hint of a gesture towards the phone girl's group. We're gonna have to watch them.

They're alright, says Frank.

More than alright, I reckon. They're damn near flawless. Perfect hair, perfect teeth. Keen as mustard, I'll bet.

Frank flashes Mo a chipped and crooked grin.

~

The clearing behind the dunes is quiet enough for Frank to hear the padding of grazing roos as the sun rises. When he emerges from the tent they scatter, regrouping at a safe distance. A big male stands tall.

Relax, fella, says Frank, soft to himself. The animal's ears twitch. Apart from the big roo's nervous mob the campground is empty. No sign of Rhys anywhere. Last Frank remembers he was plodding off away from the beach in the purple moonlight. Maybe he's got a spot over the next line of dunes.

Frank figures another day or two here and he'll be ready. He's got business down the coast. He scrapes over the ashes of last night's fire. There's a patch of warmth that's enough, with a bit of blowing, to light a little kindling. That's enough to get thin sticks burning, then an armful of more substantial stuff. Before long, he's throwing on big pieces. Smoke curls upwards without a breeze to break it until the line reaches the height of the surrounding trees. Frank breathes deep, savouring burning eucalyptus mixed with the mint bush that's growing all around, their pink flowers dotting the green. He lays two rashers, two eggs and a handful of onion rings into the spitting oil of a hot skillet.

A flock of corellas flies in to take a look, filling the branches of an old-man banksia. The bacon spatters. A billy of water simmers then breaks into a rolling boil.

Hey, smells good.

Frank almost drops the billy from its forked stick. Blimey, mate, he says. I didn't hear you coming. Kettle's boiled. D'you want a cuppa?

Don't mind. You got tea?

All I've got, says Frank. Black and smoky. He rummages in his dillybag, pulls out a second chipped enamel cup and sets it next to his own. Looks alright this morning, he says.

Eh?

Fishing. Might even catch something worth eating. Could be snapper off the point.

Rhys sips gingerly at the hot edge of his cup. Smacks his lips. Mind if I come with you? he says.

Course not, says Frank. He wraps a cloth around the pan handle and extracts his breakfast from the heat. Sometimes, he thinks, a fella just can't help but have company. I'll show you a spot I know. Rock shelf next to a deep channel. You eaten?

~

The prefects organise drinks after class in the common room. Everyone's invited.

Mo says, why not. Frank, are you in?

Sure, says Frank.

He's glad she's back. She's been crook – missed out on the role-playing session.

Dodged a bullet, she says. My guess, the prefects were right into it.

It was drama club all over, says Frank. They all wanted to be junkies.

Mo laughs. How'd they go?

Seen better, he says.

He keeps his glass full. Coke, water, Coke, water. He doesn't particularly like either. One rots his teeth. The other has no taste at all. He knows what it is he really wants. He knows where it will take him.

Mo gets caught up debating politics with the beatnik guy. Frank wanders off in search of the tutor – there's something he needs to check. But the neat lady – the one Mo calls the Dame – has the teacher's ear, and she's guarding her prize. Frank tops up with Coke again.

The business suit guys slink over. Frank's decided they're coppers though they've only ever described themselves as public servants.

Not drinkin', mate, says the overweight one.

Frank holds up his full glass, bemused.

Right. You follow the footy?

While they talk about last year's grand final Frank watches Mo. She moves easily between the groups. Even the prefects open a place for her in their tight circle and she's soon chatting away. He tries to work out how she does it. Something to do with her eyes, he reckons. She's got great eyes.

Who do you reckon? says the skinny copper.

Eh? Frank tries to reconstruct the parts of the conversation he's missed while he's been thinking about her.

At full forward – Carter or Afoa.

Carter, he says.

No way! says the fat one. He's way past his best. Gotta go with youth, he says.

While the other two argue their cases, Frank slips away. He heads for the door. His bladder is bursting. He's had enough.

~

The tide is low but turning. A small swell sweeps tassels of kelp back and forth along the edge of the shelf. Past a line of broken water the ocean drops away, deep and black. Frank's first cast fizzes through the grey morning, splashes and sinks there. He takes up the slack.

Rhys is still getting his tackle sorted. He baits his hooks with pipis collected from the beach.

Where's a good spot, d'you reckon?

Frank points across a small crescent of churned water. Try from the point there. You gotta cast over the waves. At that moment his rod tip jiggles. He slams his free hand back behind the reel as the fibreglass flexes. Line starts feeding out fast. Frank adjusts the drag. Whatever he's hooked will have its chance to run. To fight. To use what energy it has.

Told you this was a top spot.

~

You should have said goodbye, says Mo, scraping the chair back, plonking down her books.

I wanted to, but I had to go. Besides, you were talking.

Yeah. To the prefects. They don't bite. Truth is you intrigue them.

God help me, he says. You're right. I should have come over. But I had to get out. Sometimes I just… No. You're right. I should have said goodbye.

Mo says, it's no big deal. So what about tonight. Are you rushing off?

No plans, says Frank.

Good, she says, there's something I want to show you.

There's a visiting grief counsellor. She's going on and on about confidentiality. Frank starts doodling. Lines loop and twist across his page. Mo draws cartoon cats and birds. Even the prefects are getting twitchy, checking their phones and their nails. The cops excuse themselves.

The tutor can't get a word in.

… another example of this breach of the client contract …

On and on. Neat-lady scribbles every word. Mo nudges Frank. Beatnik is asleep. From where they sit they have a great view of the line of dribble sliding down his sleeve. Frank's bored, like a schoolboy.

Mo leans forward. Her shoulder-length, grey bob creates a conspiratorial curtain. Any more of this and I'll need grief counselling, she says. You had enough?

In the freedom of the corridor they breathe deep and laugh in sync.

It's been many years since Frank spent the night with a woman. He cannot remember when he last did so effortlessly, with joy and without confusion. Next morning Mo calls her boss, claiming an upset stomach. On her mantelpiece are photographs of family – growing children who have now left home, and a long-haired man wearing a green, velvet suit.

Lung cancer, she says. Eight years now. Never smoked a day in his life.

What's with the suit? says Frank

It was the 70s. What did we know?

~

By mid-morning Frank has three good snapper and a couple of pinkies. Rhys has had plenty of bites as well but he keeps losing his rig.

Show me how you're tying them, says Frank.

Frank watches him thread line through the eye twice then twist. He doubles it back through the first loop then pulls it tight, one hand holding the hook, one holding the line, and the end clasped between his teeth. The knot looks neat enough.

What do you call it? says Frank.

Call it? It's just a fishing knot. How my dad taught me.

It's a sucker knot is what it is. Are you feeling sorry for them?

Eh?

That's gonna slip with anything bigger than a sardine on the end.

Really?

Here; I'll show you. Frank cuts the line. Adds a running sinker above a sharp new hook. Watch carefully, he says.

He ties slowly but deftly, explaining each stage.

This is the most important part, he says. You've gotta take the line back through the first loop before you bring it all together. That's what locks it. It's called a 'locked half-blood'. It can't slip. Never fails.

Never?

Never, says Frank. Not if you do it properly. Here. Your turn.

~

There was this one place we used to go – me and Mum, says Frank. Back before she shot through. It was on the coast.

Mo sets down a tray – tea and Chocolate Ripples for two. Whereabouts? she says.

She called it No-name. Just a spot out east. It was two days drive back then. She said her dad discovered it. But there's a jetty so someone must have known about it once. The whole area's national park now. Lodden Inlet. But to me it'll always be No-name. The bit where we used to go, that's still just the end of an overgrown track. Pretty much unspoilt. Great fishing.

We ought to go there sometime, says Mo.

~

In the early hours Frank hears an engine starting over where the road peters out and you have walk in to reach the campsites. Next morning he checks the swale where Rhys had his swag, but there's barely a sign. The ashes of his fire have been buried. Everything straightened and tidied up. All that's left to indicate Rhys's visit is the flattened, slightly yellowing grass pressed down and starved of light.

Frank walks to the point. Dolphins in the channel break the sheen of endless, polished grey. He watches them circle back. The surface starts churning with panicked fish as the pod surrounds them. A couple of gannets join the frenzy, diving like darts into the chop, their wings tucked back.

As he watches, Frank imagines what Mo would make of it. She talks a lot about wild places. She'd have loved watching this. He'd invited her along but she'd told him he had to come alone. He'll bring her one day.

More gannets and terns enter the fray until a circle of churned white paints the ocean.

He wouldn't even be here if it wasn't for Mo. He would never have found the courage to come. He watches until the frenzy stops and the dolphins move on up the channel.

Soon he will dismantle his campsite, pack everything into the wagon and drive to the address on the scrap of paper in the glove box. He will knock on his mother's door. Even as her doorhandle turns, he will be unsure why he is standing there. But he will know he is where he needs to be. There'll be a moment – her first view of him as a grown man, his first of her since watching her wave from the end of the jetty.

Just popping into town, matey, she'd said.

From the point he can see down the beach to the inlet. The jetty where he waited as night fell. He remembers the extra snacks she left, the moon rising, wondering how long she would be, thinking about the way she was and finally understanding. He remembers the surge of hopefulness when he first heard the footsteps of the policemen she'd called to find him. He remembers their torch beams flicking through the scrub.

~

How did it go? says Mo, her voice slightly crackly on a dodgy line.

It was okay, he says. Good. You should've been there, Mo.

A tiny moment's silence follows. No voices. Just dull static before Frank corrects himself. I said that wrong. It's just you would've been … I dunno…

I'd've been happy for you, she says.

I guess that's it. We talked. We said goodbye this time, at least.

Finally… For good, d'you reckon?

Not my call, says Frank.

Fair enough, says Mo.

He wants to keep her talking – loves to hear her voice. Thinks about being back with her. Her caress – no strings attached. Her delight. Her care. The trust he has in her. Stranger still, her trust of him. There's no rush. He's over wanting things too much. Hey, I'm gonna stop off for a couple of days on the way home, he says.

At No-name? she says. Sure, love. Whatever.

Time to think, he says. Mum and all. Besides, the snapper are running.

The gambler

Nothing more than a sign, a length of cracked concrete platform and a tin shelter. Only one passenger climbed aboard. Why, in the empty carriage, he headed to the seat opposite me, I couldn't guess. He threw his bag onto the luggage rack and we took up staring out the window as the sun lowered, licking at a horizon of distant peaks.

It must have been boredom that made him speak. You're looking down on your luck, he said.

You could say.

I've ridden a lot of shaky trains to a lot of shit-hole towns. And I've seen plenty like you. No idea where you're heading.

He took a well-thumbed deck from his inside pocket. Pick a card, he said. Before I could respond he added, I don't suppose you're a drinking man.

I took a card from his fanned deck. As it happens I do have a little whisky, needs a friend, I said.

If I was to tell you you'd picked out the three of clubs – the exact card I was holding – you might offer me some of that whisky.

I pulled the bottle from my case.

He took a swig then offered it back in return for the card. What you have to understand, he said, is when you're on a losing streak your only choice is to play your way out of it, but there ain't no way to tell how long it will last. How long you been losing? He said.

The last month has been bad.

You're in trouble. He flicked the cards around in an elaborate one hand shuffle. I'll tell you a few things I've learnt, he said, reaching for the bottle. Never trust anyone. Ever. Every game is a crooked game. Every deck is stacked. That's the world.

Why you telling me this?

In answer he unfurled a grimy sheet of paper. This here, he said, is what happens when you keep away from doctors so long that when they get their hands on you they hit you with everything they've got.

Shit.

Every game's rigged. I'm holding a pair of twos against a flush. Can't bluff out of a game like that.

How long you got?

He shrugged. I'm heading north to make my peace, same place as I was born – in a field under the stars. How about another taste of that whisky?

So we hit that whisky hard, lights flashing past us in the black back-country night. And the gambler, he kept talking, like it might be the last time he ever did. Somewhere between nowhere and the morning I fell asleep against the window to his voice and the rattle of steel on steel.

I woke in the morning half-light and realised the gambler was gone. My bag was missing too. I felt my lapel, in vain, for my father's gold pin – the last decent thing I'd kept that I could hock. That's when I noticed, on the seat opposite, a poker hand fanned, face up. Five cards – all threes of clubs.

Severance

The downtown train did not, exactly, cut Martin Anderson's head off. Even if it had, Martin would have loathed the inelegance of his demise so described. He'd have resolved that split phrasal verb – relocated its dangling 'off' – before you could say boo. 'Cut off Martin's head'… pedantry perhaps, but Martin had always been a stickler. It had become a problem for him – made things worse, that need not have been made worse.

The point being, Martin's decapitation was not strictly a cutting, but rather a linear obliteration, courtesy of the crushing of a two-inch-wide strip that had once been his neck. The result was the inevitable and complete separation of the parts either side. Save for Martin's missing neck – a surprisingly complex few inches – the dismantling was clean.

Skull and jaw unharmed, brain intact, Martin – his head, to be precise – had rolled between the roaring clatter of the bogeys and come to rest, comfortably enough, one cheek against a concrete sleeper.

The evening had been cold, and as damp and miserable as would befit such a catastrophe. By 2:17am, the time of the incident, a fog had rolled in. Esther Romerez, on the last journey of a long night shift, had been concentrating on a trackside signal. She thought nothing of the barely perceptible resistance provided by Martin's neck as the first of the steel wheels mashed it. Inside her near-empty, two-car shuttle the impact was no more than if she'd collected a stray cat, or one of the local kids had put something on the tracks for the pleasure of observing its disintegration.

Only four passengers passed overhead, unaffected, or so they would have thought, by Martin, five feet below, between the tracks.

If it had been fiction – which it may well have been – the rest of Martin's story would have been the stuff about which publishers would scoff. It would have stretched credibility too far. An editor had given Martin that same feedback in response to a piece Martin had considered groundbreaking. 'The thing is, I'm not buying it. No one's going to buy it. Just give me a thread of possibility. Something to hang on to, for Christ's sake. Your ambitions for this story do not compensate for a lack of plausibility.'

That editor's name was Howard Rodman. Howard was influential on account of having at one time been the critic for a daily that had shrivelled long ago and morphed into an irrelevant, online left-wing soapbox.

Howard had jumped ship before the collapse. He'd been good with timing that way. Or lucky. A spot had opened up for him at Persephone, an energetic mid-size imprint he'd been championing in his column.

Persephone had a progressive and somewhat feminist bent and a list to match. It was within the 'up and comer' end of that list that Howard cast about, once he'd settled in the position, for writers he might mentor.

Rebecca Parkinson had been eager. Technically a solid writer, hard-working though not big on imagination, she'd accepted Howard's offer of assistance with open-eyed practicality. They'd fucked after their second meeting. Two months later Howard had stumped up for the one-bed apartment, with a view across factory rooftops to the hills she told him she loved. Rebecca started working on the first instalment of a two book deal.

Howard's wife, Alycia, admired her husband's commitment to his writers. Their trust in each other, mutually reconfirmed each morning before they left for their workplaces, had been forged on the campus battlefields of their early twenties. They had met in the thrall of resistance. Theirs was an attraction beyond mere love. They were intellectual comrades at arms.

The same fog that had shrouded Martin Anderson, and obscured him to fast-approaching train drivers, had caused Alycia's late flight to be cancelled. She'd phoned to say she'd rebooked the flight for the next day. She'd head back home on the airport bus. Howard shouldn't wait up. If he heard anything downstairs, he was not to worry. It would just be her.

Rebecca knew what time the last train ran. She slid off Howard, only slightly disgusted that he'd taken the call while she'd been attending to his increasingly unreliable erection.

She did her best, as she dismounted, to ensure her editor would be thinking of her as he raced back to his wife. Then she pushed him downstairs, before he'd had time to pull on shoes and socks, which he carried under one arm. The cold had stung his feet. A train whistle had rung in the mist. He'd run to the station. The fateful train arrived just as he reached the platform.

Three years earlier, almost to the day, Howard Rodman had encouraged Martin to redraft a manuscript plucked from the Persephone slush pile. He had, without saying it exactly, implied that Persephone would publish if Martin addressed concerns about the protagonist's voice.

At the same time as Howard was settling uncomfortably into a backwards-facing seat on Esther Romerez's train, Martin, eight miles down the line, stumbled along the edge of an embankment separating the track from the highway. Among the jumble of his many thoughts were the recurring regrets about that novel – still unpublished and now languishing on a hard drive among a drawer full of cassette tapes and forgotten stationery. The voice had been fine. It had been one of the work's strengths. Martin had spent twelve months redrafting. He'd damn near killed the story looking for a voice it never had, then salvaged it with a brilliant new twist.

In response Howard had sent a stock email – the kind Martin had been getting for years. Two contemptible sentences that amounted only to 'no'.

Howard's final interaction with Martin occurred fifteen minutes after boarding the train. He was one sock short so his left foot, cold and uncomfortable against the leather of its brogue, shook involuntarily. His hard-on was inexplicably attempting what it had resisted the whole time Rebecca and he had been working on it. A small matter that had been playing on his mind, of expenses he probably shouldn't have charged to the company, had chosen that moment to disturb him. And now this. Alycia bussing back to a house that would be empty, and the bed he and Rebecca had occupied before Rebecca had insisted a change of location might be what he needed … if he knew what she meant, which of course he did. Jesus fucking Christ. He rocketed over the spot where Martin, gaze fixed on the speed-blur of the train's undercarriage, teetered silently.

As fate – fate being the point of all this – would have it Howard managed to scramble into his apartment, sniff then straighten the sheets, wash quickly, dive beneath the covers and feign sleep just in time. He heard Alycia's key turn, and congratulated himself on his ability to manage situations.

Howard should have known – because he knew stories – that hubris has a way of arriving early. When he and Alycia made love in the dawn light of the next breaking day it would be the last time they did. Two police officers would knock soon after, asking after Mr Rodman. He'd been identified on CCTV footage that had been viewed by the one officer in the force familiar with the 'Talking Books' segment, which had run on a late-night talk show some years earlier. Fate again, so damn impossible to escape.

The footage, the officers explained, showed Howard boarding an early morning train at Wallingford Station. They wondered if he might have noticed anything unusual, as there'd been an incident.

Alycia had informed them she had no idea what it was they could be referring to. That they must have been mistaken about her husband, because he had been at home working on a conference paper. It was just an undergrad get-together, she'd said, but Howard was always happy to support young writers, whichever way he could.

The vision in the footage the officers showed her had been remarkably clear, even on the small screen of their phone. By that afternoon Howard, dismissed from the matrimonial home, had checked in to the Bayview Hotel. It had once been a haunt for artists and musicians, but seemed, when he looked around, to have become the haunt of drunks, itinerants and a few misguided backpackers.

You might think that Martin, if he'd been in a position to do so, would have appreciated this turn of events – thought Howard had deserved his misfortune. But you'd be wrong. Martin was, above all, a rational man. He had no time for the fantastic. He hated so-called magic realism with a passion. Give him Zola, Hemingway, the Russians. God, give him Austen over those weird-it-up writers Howard loved so much.

Martin did not believe in fate. Not, at least, in what it seemed to have turned into – a cosmic force, as if, having spent millennia edging towards secularism, Western society now craved its own vehicles for mad vengeance. It would have been, to him, a final injustice to think his death would trigger anything other than an eternal period of sensory nothingness.

But fate, being fate, was out of Martin's control. Most things were. When you're rolling blind-drunk and lost along a train line in the mist of someone else's neighbourhood there's little about your world you can influence. Once your head and your shoulders have been disconnected you have even less prospect of managing situations. He'd have argued that case until he was blue in the face.

Another of the riders on the train that had careered over Martin Anderson had been Dr Clinton DeJong. Clinton, like Howard, had previously crossed Martin, if not quite so closely then with more devastating consequences.

DeJong was not your average street addict. He held a professorial position that enabled him to feed his habit, predominantly, with medically sourced opiates. It was only occasionally that he ventured among the hustlers and dealers for the thrill of a dirty street score.

DeJong had been travelling back downtown after staying too long at a university function on one of the suburban satellite campuses he despised. The professor – he taught political history – had insisted he'd be good to find his own way, in spite of offers of lifts and taxis or places to stay until the morning. DeJong wasn't after anything in particular when he chose the train. He was a night person, and there was little in the world, outside a good hit, that would please him so much as the view through the window of the downtown train in the witching hour.

Unlike Martin, Clinton DeJong believed nothing happened without a reason. History had taught him that much. The reason itself – which is where the word becomes confused – need have nothing to do with logic. Things were connected, but not by such mathematical precision. Omens. Clinton accepted them absolutely. When he'd been six he'd witnessed a fight between two birds that had ended with one, a robin, pecked to death by its larger rival. A week later his grandmother, a small woman, had died. It was not the only example. He had many, some inconsequential, others ripe with import.

The mist had removed the back- and middle-grounds of Clinton's view – turned them blank and steely grey. His gaze shifted to the foreground where the overhead lamps in the carriages drew a ribbon on the rubble among which the tracks had been laid. He had been watching the abstract play of velocity and luminosity next to the train, when something momentary and dreadful caught his eye. Within the speeding field of muted white he swore he saw a body, intact to the shoulders, fall quivering beside the rails.

He rechecked this observation and found no reason to doubt it. Another man might have called the police. Clinton, no fan of law enforcement, had instead submerged into fearful conjecture about what such an apparition might mean. He had no doubt it heralded something grave.

The fear fitted precisely a growing concern he'd held about various aspects of existence. A dread had been building within him, fuelled by, among other things, latent paranoia, the imminent restructure of his faculty and falling enrolments. A joint he'd smoked before his brief presentation that night had not helped. Clinton was primed for the pessimistic interpretation of dancing headless corpses.

It was thus in a state of considerable panic that he arrived at Central and headed, not towards his apartment on the South Side but in the direction of the Bayview Hotel, where he knew he'd find a score to settle his agitation.

You'll recall that Clinton DeJong had crossed paths with the now headless Martin Anderson. The intersection of their lives had been once-removed, through Martin's eldest son. Patrick had been a nerdy, emo-ish kid, a reasonable student and, it was generally agreed, 'a thinker'. He'd scraped into DeJong's university and taken the professor's introduction to political theory.

DeJong was in the habit, in those days, of entertaining students. His unique take on liberalism led him, on occasion, to extend his hospitality to introductions to his muse. It was all self-justified bullshit, of course, but the stuff he gave them was as pure as could be found and one hit wasn't going to be the death of anyone.

Patrick Anderson liked the taste. Sought it out. Descended into its pleasure and despair.

Now, on account of an apparition, Clinton DeJong was on the search for a quick hit. He'd texted Patrick Anderson. His former student, now a resident at the Bayview Hotel, had some new gear. Patrick's stuff, in Clinton's experience was always badly cut, but not with anything too harmful.

The transaction completed, Clinton had prepared a fit in the toilet adjacent to the foyer of the hotel. The syringe was still dangling from his thigh when paramedics arrived a half-hour later.

Martin Anderson could barely have countenanced such a play of chance. His fiction, in his own opinion, was grounded in lived experience. Howard Rodman might not have seen it, but Martin's stories were anchored in a real world that was rational and concrete, and in which, if shit happened, it happened because shit happens, rather than as a consequence of some alignment of symbolically charged but otherwise un-associated elements.

Indeed, Martin would have been more inclined to regard these outcomes as simply the last lucid, story-making contortions of a vindictive writer's brain in the process of rapid de-oxygenation having been removed from its tether to the spinal cord, than to associate them with augured destiny.

Yes, that would be it. A writer to the last, Martin would have been fictionalising his memoir in order to provide the appropriate conclusion. Conclusions as it turned out. Martin had played, in the past, with multiple endings. Logic was having its way, courtesy of his failing imagination. It was creating his last fictions from the stories of his life. Perhaps all of these stories were contained within the diminishing moments between his bodily detachment and his ultimate demise.

He'd have concluded further proof of this theory if he'd been aware of a third passenger, who Martin had known only by the working name, Chantal. Martin had been, he would have admitted, at a low point when he first sought her out. For a start, Patrick had gone off the rails, straining Martin's marriage, which he valued greatly. The matrimonial tension was not helped by his inability to find a publisher for any of his three manuscripts, or to even place a short story anywhere remotely prestigious.

Martin's response had been to throw himself into new work. It's possible he had – subconsciously in his opinion – created Selena DeVille with the requirements of the research in mind. Martin understood little about prostitution. He'd found Chantal through a phone number on a flyer in a phone booth. That had been five years ago.

On the night of Martin's mortal departure, Chantal had clocked off in time to catch the last train from the tawdry suburban bolthole where she'd played temptress in a lonely man's love fantasy. She was feeling good about the world. The work night hadn't even begun. The old guy had started chatting to her at a bus stop near her sister's place. She'd sensed some easy money. They'd struck an agreement while they waited for the 212. The hotel had been the first their bus had passed.

Once inside, Chantal's client had done nothing but cry and stroke her hair, then, in the early hours, he'd paid her for the sexual works he'd imagined he'd be purchasing when he agreed she should accompany him. Better still, he'd divulged, during his miserable outbursts, both his vulnerability, and his extreme wealth. The latter was not reflected by the squalor of the room, symbolic of his unresolved self-loathing perhaps. Chantal had coaxed from him a private number, scrawled on the back of the business card of an old client of hers, and the admission that he was, in his terranean life, a judge, albeit, obviously, a poor one. He was from out of town, he told her, but not so far that they couldn't be together. She had kissed him, and returned his hair-stroking, though his locks were thin, grey wisps to her thick scarlet.

Judge Eugene William Menzies – 'Willy' was all Chantal had to know him by – was meal ticket material. He demanded only two things of her – discretion and love. That phone number was the key. He'd be used to being protected behind the arcane structures of the courts – she'd been in enough of them to know it. But those scrawled digits bypassed all that. They were his one-way ticket to Shitsville, and she was the conductor.

Martin had given her the taste for blackmail. In that sense he'd been a satisfying first course. Sex with him was like having sex with her mother, who never stopped talking. Ever. Nag, nag, nag. Because Martin was after material for some book he was writing. How do you…? What do you…? What is it like when…? In between he told her how things were with his wife, who he loved, though things were rocky. Idiot. She had a photographer snap his bare buttocks, hapless grimace reflected in the mirror above the bed to identify him to any spouse he might prefer remain unaware of the situation.

Martin had handed over ten grand to keep her quiet. Every now and then she'd contact him for a top-up. But he was strictly small-fry.

She'd pulled the same stunt on a couple of other dolts, convinced there'd be a bigger fish sniff her lure, some time. That catch had finally arrived – there'd never been anyone as ripe for fleecing as Judge Willy.

Chantal almost dozed, such was her contentment on the journey home, the gentle roll of the carriage and the lateness of the night. The judge's priceless contact was tucked in her handbag on the seat beside her. She hadn't noticed the loose clasp. The bag had fallen open and, while Chantal dreamt of wealth, the precious number, dislodged by the rocking train, had teetered perilously on a thin edge of leather.

That's where it would have stayed until she gathered it up at the end of her journey had not the wheel over which she was sitting jagged slightly at the resistance of the remains of Martin Anderson's cervical vertebrae. The vibration, though dampened by the train's suspension, was enough to cause the bag to jump a little, the card to topple out, and for Chantal to wake from her reverie, realising her station was fast approaching. She lifted the bag by both handles and readied to depart. The judge's number slid down between the upright and bench sections of her seat, fluttered onto the floor and landed in a sticky puddle of cola.

Martin would have been beside himself. Not that he'd have minded Chantal receiving her comeuppance. But three passengers, three connections, three lives altered in accordance with an apparent supernatural conjunction – it was too much. Too much, honestly, for a sceptical oxygen-starved brain, rapidly cooling in the outer urban frost.

Martin might have been relieved to discover that the last of the four riders on Esther Romerez's train was a woman he had never met.

Which was, unfortunately, not to say their paths hadn't crossed. Francesca Clover had thrown in her job at a high-end fashion house to pursue a love of writing. Martin knew that story. Starry-eyed up-and-comer. A couple of breaks. A face the press could love. A natural on social media, by virtue of a vacuous and acritical demeanour. She'd developed a profile without ever putting in the hard yards.

He may not have known her but he knew her story.

Martin had been on the shortlist for a spot in a prestigious residency program. On the afternoon of his demise he'd received the email he'd been dreading and sweating on in equal part. His index finger wavered on its way to the Enter key. He swallowed hard.

Francesca Clover didn't need the residency. Just as she hadn't needed the fashion job, her father's convertible Mercedes, the rollcall of notable boy- and girlfriends. Francesca needed nothing. Her family was descended from the Clover Brewery clan. She could afford to do whatever took her fancy. She could afford to write, or not to write. She could afford the light-weight, chick-lit flippancy that had caught the judges' attentions.

'Oh, look,' she'd said when her email arrived, spinning her phone for her lunch companion to see. And when she'd opened it, and her place in the program was confirmed, they toasted her with good French champagne.

Martin imagined the transformation the residency could give him – introductions into the inner sanctum of a major publisher. Time to do nothing but write. A guarantee, at least, that his manuscript would be read. It might help appease Christine, who was over being the breadwinner for his unacknowledged creative brilliance. He lowered his finger, then waited for the message to download, like a condemned man anticipating a miracle intervention.

Francesca Clover had never been big on detail – another thing she could afford to overlook. She had skimmed the 'good character' fine print in the residency's application. The donor had been both literate and puritanical, but Francesca thought little of it, or the cocaine possession charge her father's lawyers would be dealing with in a couple of weeks. Her family was on tennis playing terms with Judge Menzies, who'd been listed to hear the case.

Francesca was not unfamiliar with late-night trains. She had discovered a couple of bars, out in these industrial suburbs, where she could escape the wealth she part loved and part loathed, and meet, if things worked out, men who did not place her on a chart of old family ties. Her evening had not gone quite as she'd hoped. A trucker with no stomach for liquor had let her down. No matter. She rode back towards her city apartment, content.

She'd not have been so happy if she'd known that Judge Menzies' disposition was about to be altered by an unfulfilled rekindling of desire – the unfortunate by-product of a misplaced phone number. The object of his passion was nodding off in the next carriage, the judge's number on a card on the edge of the handbag beside her.

The digits on the clock of the new millennium's destiny spun even more precisely than the old hands of time, and just as irrevocably. Within milliseconds of each other the two women – strangers on a lonely train – sped over the diminishing resistance of Martin Anderson's desiccated throat.

Francesca's story would take a little while to play out. Judge Menzies waited beyond a week for a call from his loved one. His demeanour became acerbic. Having had his pledge of ardour so callously disrespected, and at heart an old-school misogynist, he had no time, by the afternoon Francesca Clover's case came before him, for silly women and their excuses.

Her family money ensured coverage of the case in the media. Francesca avoided jail time, but scored an unwanted conviction and a community order helping intolerable special-needs children. She never did take up the residency offer and her invitations within society circles dried up, from B-list to somewhere well below C.

Publishers looked elsewhere for the next sassy voice; the next semi-autobiographical musing on contemporary young urban professional womanhood. None of that was of any consequence to Martin, whose boat, as they say, had long since sailed.

It would have been hard not to see the possibility, at least, of the hand of some connected power in the conjunctions of people and events that had followed Martin Anderson's neck being mangled by the last train of the night. He'd always despised coincidence. It was too easy. The stuff of bad fiction, too removed from the reality he'd sought to capture. Too frustrating. The near-dead Martin would have been out of his mind.

It was so unfair. Everything else during the day leading up to his decapitation had been perfect. Another rejection email he'd believed, too much, he would not receive. The signs of his marriage disintegrating. The last straw. Looking for someone – someone else – to blame. The argument with his son. Then out-of-town, not really understanding how he'd come to be in a rough neighbourhood. The bar at which he'd drunk more than his fill. A fight with locals avoided, but narrowly. Thrust out, alone into the frosty morning. A long, long way from home. All great stuff. All grist for the gritty realist's slowly grinding mill.

But the post-script – had he seen it coming – would ruin everything. These characters. These stories. The connections that could never have been plotted so precisely. And now his last hope – that the stories might be the product of a dying fictional intellect seeking revenge – seemed undermined. Francesca's story did not fit this rational frame. He'd known nothing of her. Nothing, at least, until now, which hardly counted, being after (or at least at the very moment of) his apparent death. But she deserved, as much as the others, to contribute to rebalancing the scales of destiny she'd helped tip against him. And such … it was so infuriating … such, it appeared, had been her fate.

These thoughts filled Martin Anderson's head. They were his last mortal vestige.

Ambulance officer Oscar Knezic snapped on a second pair of gloves. He shone his flashlight just long enough to locate something to latch on to. A hank of Martin's hair.

Martin might have approved, at least, the dramatic pause, the effort Oscar took to slow his breath, still his heartbeat. But it was too late. In Oscar's beam a face set in abject disapproval mocked him momentarily. He shivered. Martin Anderson's head was … fucking … what was that? Scowling at him. That's what it was. Holy Jesus.

In that instant Oscar knew he'd lost the heart for jobs like that. He reached quickly.

Doing his best to ignore the churn of that night's hamburger and Coke, he found purchase in Martin's blood-matted locks. In a flash he'd hoisted Martin's head from its sleeper pillow and thrust it, sour expression first, into a heavy, black, polythene bag, which he tied tightly up.

What you might find

I ndi had been given the lucky dip. Not particularly inspiring, but, as always, she put her heart into it. She'd made it up in a plastic rubbish bin and packed the donated treats—trinkets and lollies, vouchers for ice-creams and hot dogs—in little boxes from the factory in town. Then she'd buried them under strips of paper—shredded documents that had once been important and confidential. Now they were meaningless … perfect for concealing. The whole thing looked as pretty as a picture. Early sun breaking through light cloud cover gave the marquee-covered 'big oval' the look of something enchanted and medieval. If you squinted a little or used your imagination.

She had her back turned, drawing a sign on daisy-shaped card, when Don wandered past looking for somewhere to put the pieces from a 'bit of an accident' they'd had with some jars from the jam stall.

The exquisite leaf

Walter Chang knew, as soon as he opened the door, that they'd been again and they'd keep returning until they had what they were seeking. Not much was disturbed except the smell of the room. The teak shelves and cabinets that hid every inch of wall stood just as always, as did the tins and jars of tea of every exotic kind. There was a particular smell that came from the room being undisturbed at night and the first breath of it each morning was all he needed to convince him to drag his aching bones through another day of measuring, tasting and selling.

He came as usual from the temple on the hill. As soon as he opened the shop door he knew the portents had been right. The strangers had been back.

Chang's had survived through three generations, through revolutions, wars, extortion rackets, economic highs and lows and times when it seemed no one valued the teas on his shelves and the business would die with its aging customers. But new generations would discover the subtle beauty and when they did Chang's had always been there for those seeking the finest and the strangest.

Most of his teas were sold fresh or aged briefly. But there were a few that were kept like fine red wines. Some were pre-revolutionary, picked in the days of the Europeans, compressed into tight inky dark wheels like hashish and wrapped in leaves and string, they were the teas of connoisseurs, rare in every sense and extremely valuable.

Chang went to the safe. This time it had been opened. They'd taken some of his best. But they hadn't found what they'd been after. The safe was his last line of protection. They would not be so discreet next time. Walter Chang felt beneath the countertop of a cabinet his great-grandfather had made. He found the wooden latch that released the secret panel and the drawer within it. Inside was a single century-old 24-inch wheel of the finest aged tea ever picked and pressed. It was the only one in existence, rumoured more than known. He knew exactly what he would do. He had been imagining this day. With the tea in a simple calico bag he headed for the train station. By afternoon he would be at the house of his most valued customer.

Zhou was a collector as well as an aficionado. He would be prepared to pay any amount for the tea. But he would pay Walter only a cup made from a few of the leaves scraped from the edge of the wheel. They would drink together, for that was what tea was for. Then they'd re-wrap the wheel. Their single taste would suffice for the rest of their lives. For Walter that would not be so long, for that tea, his grandfather had told him, would be his family's curse and their salvation. Zhou would see that Walter's grandchildren, who drank only coffee and Coca-Cola and knew nothing of the exquisite leaf, would be well looked after. Walter would taste what had been forbidden so long and then he would be prepared for another life. This was how he had always known it would be.

Rollin'

Three and five. Hansy scoops the dice just as Dee comes in. Evens, he thinks. So I'm leaving. Evens I go, odds I stay. He turns the ivory-cold cubes around in his palm. He runs his thumb along the rounded edges.

'Careful with those things.' Dee laughs but eyes him sideways.

'No worries, love. Just muckin' round.'

That's what he'd said when he lost the house. He still didn't know how she'd had the courage to stay. He was just mucking around. He wouldn't be going anywhere in a hurry.

Best out of three he thought, sending the dice tumbling across the coffee table.

The Game

The priest is brought in by the screws for my entertainment. Or theirs. Buck tooth smile and mad sandy hair. Rose-pink cheeks. Fidgety like he's not sure why he's here. So it's me has to come up with an opening line. Grand days, I say, because irony seems to suit the scene.

Oh, aye, he says. Grand indeed, with the Lord so close at hand.

Can't help what you can't help, I say.

Tis only prayin' and forgiveness can help the helpless, he says. And faith. Blessed above all things.

All things? I say.

Aye, and that's the truth.

Faith, the truth? Which came first?

'Twas the word came first. In the beginning…

God before faith, then.

God is faith, he says, which means nothing, if you ask me. You can think too much about it, I says. Tie yourself in knots.

Not faith, he says. Faith is pure and simple.

Like all the best excuses, I say.

The father tries to hide a sneer.

~

Time ticks slow on such nights. I need something to help it pass. We're all talked out on faith. Stalemate. Proves my point. Faith gets you nowhere. I need something to count the minutes down to zero. So I suggest a few rounds of 'hangman' on the cell walls – the ponderous minutes could do with levity.

Hangman, he says. I suppose you think you're funny. But he agrees to play.

His words are predictable. Godly and redemptive. The first one I guess before we start but let the play proceed, scratching the game into the softest part of the stone wall, near the bunk where the damp is worst. I allow him just a glimpse.

S A _ V _ T _ _ _

But a glimpse is all. After those I choose 'd' and 'r' and 'e' to build the scaffold higher. I choose 'p' and 'c' and 'd' and draw the dangling stick-man in the noose.

The priest sweats over the schoolroom pastime. He wants the word that I will not give him. He wants my intervention to provide it. So much for his faith.

~

Outside, a cock crows. The Lord's own rays of warming sun sneak through the high bars. Footsteps slow on the old stones – not quite a march. Reluctant but deliberate regardless. Key turning. Locking barrels disengaging. The warden slides his greasy face through. Time you were on your way, Father, he says. And he winks my way, which is what petty power looks like in a shithole like this.

The man of God blesses me one last time.

The door closes on me as it has every morning of these last seven years. Through the bars I hear the clomping footfall of the warden and his men and the man of the cloth calling out now, barely coherent, proclaiming his innocence in the eyes of God.

... but it falls

An ancient stringybark marked the bottom of the property, where the creek used to be – it hadn't run in years.

Harry and Carmel survived the dry years too. The drought was hard enough. As debts mounted Harry hit the bottle. At his lowest he'd hit her too. Isolated on theirs parched acreage with the dams empty and their few remaining sheep agisted they bunkered down through five dry years.

If it hadn't been for Clayton the place would have been lost. He'd looked in whenever he could. Found jobs for Harry too. They rebuilt the fence between their places. Clayton set Harry up with the free-range turkeys that helped get them through.

When a week of rain filled the dams Clayton came to celebrate. Harry drank too much and passed out. Carmel and Clayton talked through the stormy night.

In the morning the stringybark was down, its shrunken roots useless in the mud. It hadn't been the hard times that had made it vulnerable, but the slackening that followed.

Particle physics

My sister arrived, at last, at the Library of all Notions, in a kingdom of peaks and low white cloud. Behind heavy doors, in disappearing rows, were the volumes that held the knowledge of the world. She went instinctively to the furthest corner. Breathed the mustiness of time. Sunbeams played above the shelves. As she reached for her answer she understood and it no longer mattered that the book's only words – your search is your purpose – turned to dust in the act of peeling back the vellum.

The Heracles train

Heracles regarded the heavens, disconsolate, for another quest was complete yet still he failed to please Olympus. The mortal edge at which he had arrived appeared beach-like, immateriality lapping in a shimmer onto the land. He had an urge to view what was beneath, so lay flat on the sand and leant forward.

Hera, watching as always, observed the part of him that extended beyond the world cease to be.

For Heracles himself the sensation was of weight and mass and energy reaching only to those parts of his body that remained. Beyond these, where his head and his fingertips had been, was blind consciousness.

He had endured many hardships. The new sensation, of nothing that could be seen or touched, excited him. Without a thought he edged forward, neck then shoulders gone, then chest. He found purchase on the sand and pushed towards where zero and infinity were indistinguishable, where now was all-of-time and peace as absolute as the absence of peace. He let himself slide into it. At the last moment, as he struck out beyond his embodiment, the buckle of his sandal caught on a length of vine. First the vine, then its roots and the things ensnared by them trailed him towards nothing and the world he'd honoured with his bravery began slowly dragging itself, each small part connected, piece by piece into oblivion.

Green

The Belleview Street place had been a share-house. Daniella bought it in spring. By mid-summer, when she moved in, vegetables were flourishing in the backyard and nectarines hung, plump and enticing from the tree in the corner. The tomatoes and beans she ate wouldn't have been planted when she bought the place – she remembered the freshly tilled soil.

Pinned to the noticeboard in the pantry she found a hand-written planting guide – meticulous notes added over the years with rotations for each bed and each season. The tomatoes came out in February. She dug in manure, planting silverbeet after a couple of weeks. Her first harvest was in late March. She rang the agent who'd handled the property. 'I've got mail for them, do you have a forwarding address?'

Before she finished parking, she spotted him. He was lanky and handled his spade with ease. His eyes flashed at her as she approached him. They were as deep green and seductive as the leaves in her basket.

Post

There was a note on the door when Eric got home. Dinner's in the fridge. Don't wait up. It's over. It wasn't much of a goodbye. He unpinned it and put it in the draw where he kept love letters and mementos. He found the meal – sausages and mash – then sat alone on the couch to eat. When his favourite TV show finished he went to bed, lying as usual on the side near the window, listening until sleep overtook him.

Next morning during breakfast he put pen to paper. Darling, forgive me. We can work things out. He slipped the note into an envelope. On his way to work he dropped it into his letterbox, where it would be waiting for him at the end of the day.

Persona

I cannot move so I cannot touch. Only be touched, which is not the same. My limbs do not respond to my desires. My body resists. All I have is my voice, and, now, this machine that writes what I say. It heeds my commands. I tell it to send my messages to you. It sends them. And I wait.

You respond, describing our intimacy.

I tell the machine what to write back.

We are responding each to the other. Our words touch, stroke, explore. Our words admire.

Our words deceive.

Bidding farewell I rise and stretch. I make a sandwich then log on again. Another site. Another fiction. Your message describes what I cannot see.

Bush burial

Shovels | Oh, yeah – I know what shovellin' sounds like | Three hours | crunch, scrape, flmp | Hutchy behind me mutterin', 'dig, bastard, dig' | An' now, this | An' this forever | He won't be happy | 'No-one'll know,' 'e said | 'Nice and deep,' | 'Respectful, like … harder to find'

Cos 'e couldn't do nothing | I fucked up | What's a fella like Hutchy to do? | Sure I pleaded | Hutchy was cool | He listened to me | He heard me out | 'Hutchy, we're mates' | 'You an' me, Hutch, you an' me'

How long's it been? | One year, ten, twenty | No more than that – old bones strong but no flesh | Ten I reckon | No memories, just … imprints | Cos there are things … like the roos | Thump, thump, thump, goin' down the hill | Thump, thump, thump, bouncin' up | No respect for the dead

An' cars on the road | They ain't never fixed it | Still bad like when me and Hutch came down | Everythin' shakin' and rattlin' | Gives me the tremors | So you get to know, but there's no time | No buildin' one moment on the last

The girl was a mistake | Made things messy | I felt her lying underneath me | Soft but cold she was | Cold like before | 'Cush' I called 'er | Eh, Cush, how's it goin'? | Flesh turned to dirt | She's gone | I still think, though, sometimes | You an' me, Cush … ya gotta laugh | She touched me once | A finger bone, maybe, slippin' around in the clay | How long? | A second, a day, a week, a year? | But she's not there now

But I do remember before | Like at school | Hutch was the one | Them teachers didn't stand a chance | You, Hutchinson, and your mate, you'll never 'mount to nothin' | They never seen the Bentleigh job | Hutch was brilliant | An' down at Wonthaggi that time, the bottlo | They never seen that

Oh, yeah | We coulda done Parkville | It was all there | I remember | Had to hide out | Fine at first and then … cops everywhere | But Hutch was cool | No guns, nothin' | Knew them hills better than any of 'em | And then … the farmhouse in the valley | Food an' a car he says | The girl got in the way | I shouldn'a done it

Right here | Who could know? | Only Hutch | Hutch? | It's you | Ain't it? | Quiet | Nothin' | Restin' | Yeah – hard work diggin' | I remember | Three hours | Dig, bastard, dig | An' her all the while shakin' | An' you, Hutchy | Cool | Stop ya squirmin' | An' me never knowin' | An' thinkin' we'll be right with 'er out of the way | An' you shoutin' | Dig, bastard, dig

Hutchy? | Closer | How long's it been? | You came back, Hutch | Careful now | Don't smash me up, Hutch | Don't break me | Did ya know, Hutch? | Still alive … the worst thing | An' her too, squirmin' | An' the big clods | An' the light goin' | An' air goin' | An' ribs cavin' in | An' taste an' smell | An' then … this | An' now …

… clods comin' off | weight comin' off | like my ol' mum – I remember – liftin' the blankets | Peeling 'em one by one in winter | Wake up, fella … time fer breakfast | An' me under there, an' piss on the sheets an' Da' givin' me a hidin' | Real close now

Hang on, Hutch… | Someone's there | Rattlin' bones – cars 're comin' | You hav'n' got time | Quick | Ya gotta go | Hutch? | What 're ya doin'? | No, Hutchy, don't mix us up, mate | Me an' her | I dunno… | Don' break us, mate | Careful Hutch

—Darryn James Hutchinson—

Eh?

—Darryn James Hutchinson? —

Coppers!

—Back off, Hutchinson | Put it down | Hutchinson | Put down the spade | Drop the bag. —

Floating

Crack | Revolver—one—two | Shotgun—three—four | Revolver—five—six—seven

Seven … bastards | Fallin'… fallin'… sack 'n all | An' 'er | An' you too | Crashin' down | You an' me Hutch | Together | Like ol' times | I knew it, Hutch | An' me in the sack with 'er now | All mixed up | All fucked up

An' Dad in the backyard | Way back | Way back I remember | Dig, bastard, dig

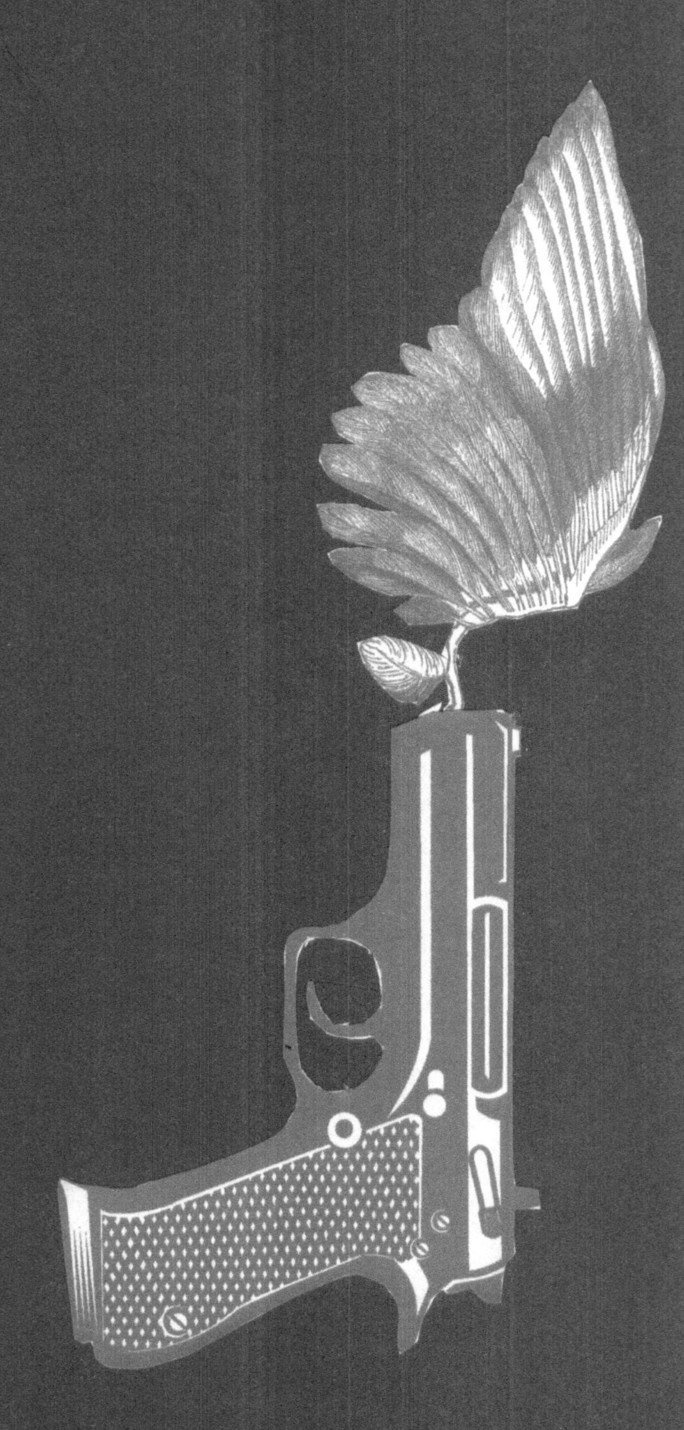

Tomorrow is a village far away

At the bottom of our apartment block is a playground, but it's mostly used by the gangs.

Not today though. There's been trouble. Ambulances came last night. The police – they usually stay well clear – are here in force.

The stairwell smells of stale piss and we're glad to reach the sun-battered concrete of the compound.

I sit on one end of the see-saw and Oscar on the other. We bounce slowly up and down as we talk about leaving this place. We've had word from Oscar's uncle. Tomorrow we catch the bus to his village. We will live with his family in the hills where there are no gangs. Oscar will help with the animals and the crops and I will help in the kitchens and take care of the little ones. Perhaps we will have a family of our own. We will be poor but safe.

A policeman approaches across the yard. 'Papers,' he calls, waving his revolver.

We pull our battered documents from our pockets. As he's checking them a single shot rings out. The policeman leaps behind a swing. My eyes shoot to Oscar. He seems unharmed. Only then do I breathe. Warm liquid rushes into my lungs where only air should be.

In the Saturday magazine

There's a piece in the paper about Laura. She was young when I knew her, always wanting to race the wind, to crash through. Like she crashed through me.

Laura. My first girlfriend.

What would she say if she knew I'd never forgotten? I wonder. The article says she has a partner now – a theatre director. That's him in the messy suit, standing behind her, in the background. Laura looks focused, the way I remember. She's a bit fuller in the face perhaps, but the same dynamite figure. The same determination. She's living a high-flying corporate life and she's just been appointed dean of a new design school.

The article teases out the influences on Laura's career. *There are few things Laura Illingworth regrets*, it says, *though she admits to mistakes in her early relationships…*

'I sometimes wish I could go back and explain my restlessness, because I didn't know how much I was hurting people I actually cared about,' she says. She recalls her first great love. 'It was seventeen years ago…'

I do the sums. My pulse quickens.

'… a boy called…'

But it's not me. The one she left me for perhaps. How brittle I must be. How shallow to feel this scrap of the past so deeply.

The line

This morning the second-half goal is the only story in town. The network boss wants an angle on the story. Something no one else has. No senile old referees banging on, he says.

Lardner pipes up, though these days he's about as far down the pecking order as you can get before you're out the door, so usually keeps his thoughts to himself. I've got something, he says.

Someone mutters, This'll be good.

Not an angle, he says. The angle. I've got the angle.

Ah, the prodigal son. Simon Georgiou, Head of Sport, tosses a Tic Tac into his mouth as he eyes his former colleague. Georgiou goes through two packs of the little mints a day. They won out over cigarettes after thirty hard years covering everything from tiddlywinks to Olympics. We've seen your angles before, Marcus. It was angles got you where you are today. So let's hear it. What angle, exactly, do you have?

All the way along the line, says Larsen. Clear view. On my phone – I got it all.

Bullshit. Georgiou straightens. No one's got that. The broadcasters all missed it – cameras in the wrong spots. And you're telling me it's in your pocket.

No shit, big boy.

Jesus.

So … goal or not? says Lisa Rickards. Her *Sport Desk* show goes to air in an hour.

But before Marcus Lardner can answer her, Georgiou is re-organising things around the unseen footage. My office, now, Marcus. Lisa, we'll get you something … make some room … drop the bloody-figure skating. The rest of you get ready to ride this one.

Then, with Georgiou's door shut and the sudden buzz of the newsroom behind them, Marcus gets to answer Lisa's hanging question, though Lisa's not there to hear. It's just him and the big guy. Marcus half-thinks he should spin this out, because it's been a while since anyone paid him attention. He's been on thin ice since the scandal – better to not get too smart.

Goal? Georgiou makes a grab for Marcus phone.

Oh yeah – no doubt.

Fuck, says Georgiou. Fuck'n fuck.

What? This is a great story.

Really? You never did get how this works, did you, Marcus? It's only a good story, says Georgiou. I need great. 'Lineswoman Got It Wrong' – now that would have been a great story. Georgiou's focus shifts to a blank space in the scruffy cavern of his office. He raps his knuckles on the edge of his desk. Show me that fucking footage.

~

Lisa gets 'Doubts About Cup Goal Grow' as the headline for her show. But that's it. Just the same footage everyone has seen a hundred times even if her script predicts new evidence. She knows the main story's being held back and polished up for the evening boys to run.

~

The Cup final is the biggest game of the season, made more so by the two city teams, lining up against each other. The Wolves are working-class survivors and old-school brawlers. The Fury are as new and polished as their silver and gold home strip – a commercial monolith created by the league and loaded with flash, cashed-up internationals with silky skills and attitudes to match. Their passionate crowd is younger. To the supporters of the old clubs they're ignorant of the traditions of the game and inclined to revel in their own arrogance. Many of those fans have only come recently to the game.

Early goals have the teams tied at the break. In the second half the Wolves push hard, running the Fury ragged. But Fury's Iranian goalkeeper is impassable, pulling off a string of stunning saves. As the clock ticks towards full-time the structures of both sides loosen. They surge forward at every opportunity, desperate for the goal that will break the deadlock.

Finally, two minutes into extra time, Fury's Argentinian striker gathers a speculative long pass on the edge of the box, turns the only defender who has scrambled back to stop him, and unleashes. The ball tracks towards the top right corner of the net, but seems reluctant to drop. When it reaches the line the top of the ball cannons into the bar redirecting it groundwards. It bounces and the spin created by the impact with the bar is enough to redirect it back towards the Wolves' relieved keeper, Reynolds.

But when Reynolds looks up to clear the ball – his thoughts on extra time, perhaps penalties after that – he sees the ref, with his hand up, racing for the sideline where the lineswoman is indicating the striker's ball has crossed the line.

Players rush the officials. Both managers and their benches join them. The roar from the stands builds – an amorphous crescendo as joy and anger crash against each other. Triumph and despair. The officials are not swayed. They have made their decision.

Police and security push through the milling players. The referee points to the centre of the ground, confirming the score. Within a minute of a confused restart – the ground still fizzing with barely withheld passion – he blows time.

That evening violence and lawlessness erupts in the streets of the suburbs surrounding the arena. Shops are burnt and looted. A group of Fury supporters is set upon.

~

When the sport channel starts promoting the footage to be aired on their evening bulletin, Donna Leslie fears she might vomit again, as she did three times after the game the night before.

The memory of her trip home is a blur. Flashing lights and white-hot anger. Streets full of young men intent on a kind of justice that neither rulebooks nor lawbooks understand. The police car in which she was hidden took a buffeting. If those outside had known she was behind the car's dark-tinted glass, who she was, what she had done to their team, they would have done more than taunt and rock and bang flat hands and balled fists onto the panels. They would have done more than climb on the hood. Clamber on the roof. Jump on it until it started to buckle.

She has suffered migraines before but nothing like the blinding incessant beast that has wrapped her in these hours. And yet she cannot and will not try to sleep. Every flicker of energy she can find goes into replaying the moment. Each time she does she feels the certainty of it, now so much in doubt that she barely trusts herself to breathe.

And yet that split second was exactly what she had worked so hard for. Fought for as if nothing else was important. She had climbed the ranks from the juniors, amateurs, local leagues into the minor divisions, taking every opportunity, turning nothing down. It was easier for others. She knew that. But however hard the climb would be for her, she'd always told herself she would succeed. Her grandfather had officiated at three World Cups. When she'd been twelve years old she'd promised him that she would do the same. That night he'd given her a battered old matchbox, her most treasured possession now. His whistle.

Donna's hand had been clenching so tight around it that its outline was marked on her palm by the time the evening bulletin started. She did not have long to wait to see what had been promoted as startling new evidence. Grainy footage but stable enough to be useful. From his seat on the front row of the second tier Marcus Lardner had had a clear view of the goal mouth. The section of fence on which he'd leant his phone had stabilised the image.

Donna saw what she had seen from the sideline the evening before – the long ball coming in, the trap and spin and strike. The ball like a bullet. When it clanged against the crossbar she imagined the sound it had made.

But the next part was wrong. Disconnected from what she'd told herself she knew. The network slowed the footage down. The shape of the ball emerging from behind the post but never entirely, as she'd been sure it had. As it bounced the broadcaster zoomed in, slo-mo, then paused at the point where it was clear the ball had not completely crossed the line. It was still obscured by the post. Not a small part either. Enough for the coterie of experts that followed to declare that the official had made their call in error.

Donna Leslie lurched forward, the bile that was all that remained in her stomach emptying into the bucket she had kept close beside her.

~

Marcus burst into Georgiou's office. What have you done with my fuck'n footage? What have you done with my story?

Your story? says Georgiou.

That was my footage. You … you… Marcus Lardner searches for a word.

Fixed it, arsehole. Gave it to Post-Production. Got em to work their magic on it. Turned it into a story with legs. What do you think?

Peeling away

I came across a lonely billboard with its top layer half peeled off. It read: Jesus Christ, pure indulgence. I went in search of its meaning.

Traditional churches turned me away. The religious fringes beckoned. The image of the deity in sacred robes and black stockings drove me on. Drawn at last to the town of Parchment. I came to the Church of the Angel of Redemption.

You were coming down as I was going up. Those legs, those stockings, the feline grace as you took the steps, half sideways in your heels. You were the one. Pure indulgence, I repeated. I turned.

When I caught up to you, in the afternoon sunshine, on the stubbly main road of Parchment, you told me I'd been right to follow. 'He works in mysterious ways,' you said. We went away together. For three years we built our life around your strangeness. But this morning you were gone.

Suddenly adrift, I caught a bus back to the place where I'd read the message that had guided me to you. But all that remained, beside the highway, were the last shredded pieces of something too faded to mean anything at all.

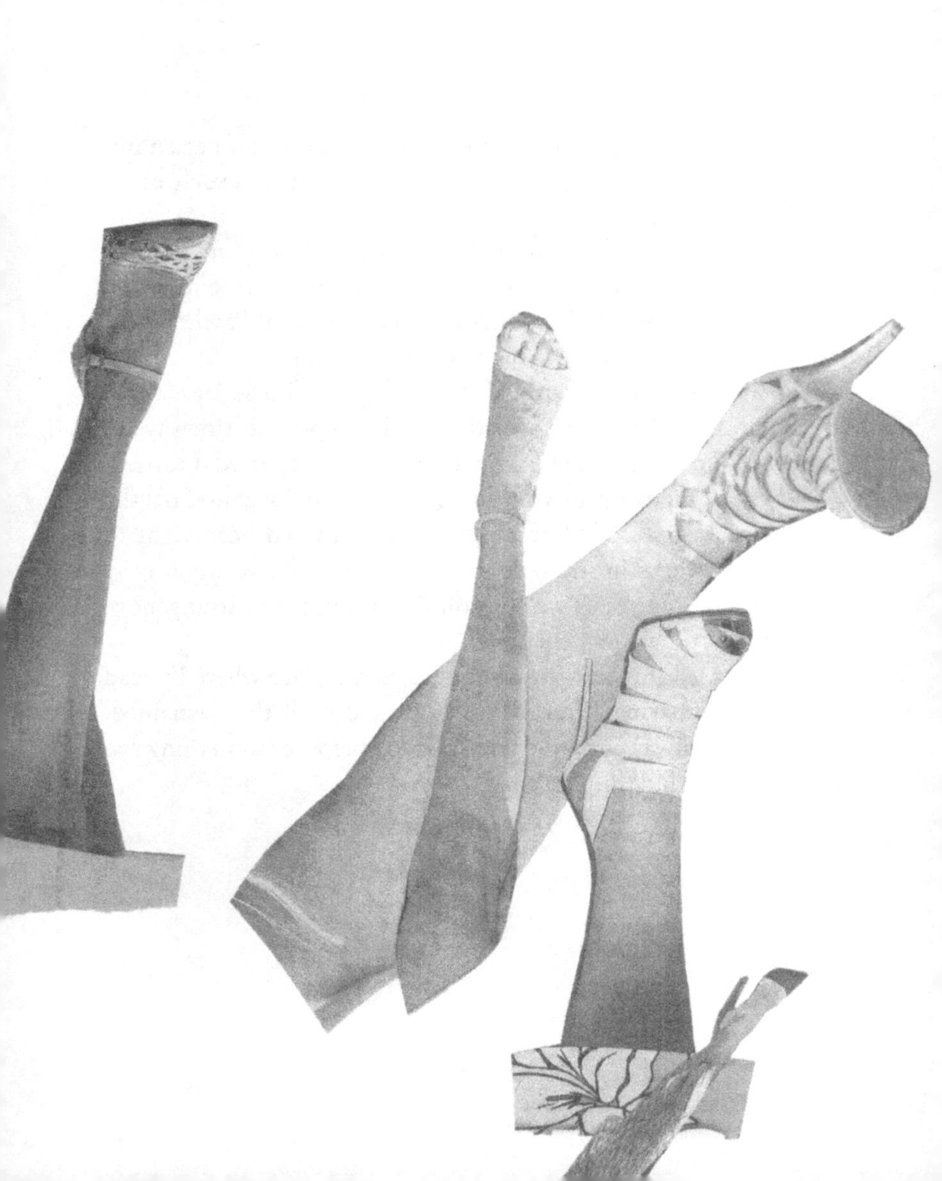

Rescued

Search crews found him on a rock ledge trying to sing. It was something else he'd forgotten. That and his past – growing up, old girlfriends and all the years with me – wiped clean.

At first there was high farce to our tragedy. 'Robert, you say?'

I'd nod.

'I don't remember.'

'I know, darling,' I'd say. 'I know.'

Later, when he understood, he'd get annoyed if he thought I was trying to feed him memories – old songs, photos, anything. So I banished them. The house became blank in their absence.

Until, on my way home one evening, I detoured via the shops. I tried on shoes, bought new stockings and sampled perfume offered by a girl with a rock-hard smile.

When I walked into the house he sat up. I'd taken to pecking him on the cheek as if he remembered. As I did he breathed long and hard, smelling the new scent. Suddenly memories began cascading from him.

They weren't of me.

I accepted them, regardless.

The only word she had for it

Love. That's what Mish called this thing she had with Clay.

They spent their days riding the trains, drinking canned spirits. When they were out-of-it they were invincible. They sprawled and brawled and cursed. People moved away as if they had a force field about them. Nothing could touch them.

On a day in winter like every other they spread their bags across the back seats of a crowded city-bound tram. Business people in suits and pressed skirts glanced sideways.

''Ere, lady.' Clay sharpened his eyes on a middle-aged woman. ''Ave a seat. 'Ave a drink.'

'No, thank you.'

'Too good f'rus?' He and Mish shared a laugh like a sneer.

The woman flushed.

'I said, too good f'rus?' Clay let fly with a spray of abuse that counted, in his mind, for humour.

Things happened in a rush after that. A tall man hauled Clay up by his collar. Screaming, Mish took a fingernail gouge from the stranger's arm. Clay found the knife he used sometimes at convenience stores. One thrust. Two. Not deep. More men came forward, overpowering him. Screaming. Blood on seats. Then sirens.

Her boyfriend on the floor, a foot planted hard on his neck. Mish spitting threats as they dragged her away.

She called it love. The only word she had for it.

Paperback

I didn't come here to be accosted. Your mask covers nothing. You play the fool for fools and tourists. You bumble through your two-bit show with the grace of a Shakespearean hack. All the misplaced bravura. But to me you're plain selfish, grabbing my arm like a madman. Dragging me after you, sniggering at my protests. Cheap laughs for the watching crowd that parts for us. I find myself at the centre of its gleeful ring. A streetlight flickers.

Encircled, I become the unwitting prop for your haranguing. And, yes, if I was part of the circle, or even just in a relaxed frame of mind, I might find some amusement at my own expense. But I'm not. Okay. I am not part of your performance. I'm not a prop. A sidekick. I'm not in the mood. If I was – in the mood, I mean, for crap like yours – would I be wandering around the night market by myself so close to midnight.

The air is warm. It is the hour for lovers and loners.

Okay?

I'm not here because I want your attention. I want fresh air and a good book or two to take home. All I ever take home with me these days.

And no, I don't care about the stupid curse you're casting on me now, making them laugh as I pull away. I don't care that the No Fun Bird will peck out my eyes as I sleep.

So fuck off back to drama school and leave me alone.

With this curse I score laughs of my own. Your crowd's sympathies shift. It splits allowing me to mark a respectable retreat.

I do not turn back. I seek the darkness of the mass of bodies. The anonymity I was after when I came here. The bustle in which to lose myself. I push through to the booksellers by the river. The stories they sell, which talk to me without making demands. They want only that I should want them. They wait in their battered paper covers for me, peeping guiltily from between the august, respectable volumes that demand attention – hardbacks expecting confirmation of their leather-bound superiority, and oversized tomes with pompous titles. Stupid books that expect a reverence marked by how they are picked up, held, turned over.

Not me. Sorry. I toss those aside. They hold no appeal.

Among these turgid tomes there is even one I recognise. Slightly battered, as well it should be. His book – *The Poets of Romance*. I recognise the spine before I read his name and I cannot help the flush of this knowledge – the deep unreasonable want that triggers an underutilised chain of synapses to leap from printed words to imagined sheets drawn across the two of us together. But the words, the ink, the nasty vinegary smell of too-freshly remaindered pages disgusts me. I throw him back with the others; the professors and experts; the celebrities and self-opinionated proselytisers.

I need old paper covers. Cheaply made for late nights and furtive dreams, soft between the fingers with a wood-pulp texture that rasps on aroused fingertips. No gloss.

No decent book was ever printed that was too large to secrete in a coat pocket. Too solid to roll the cover back. I need the singular linger of letterpress ink. Stories that smudge across the pages. They don't write them like that anymore. I need cruel men and bad women, criminal intent and fate closing in. Fast. I need the kind of moral hopelessness avoided in the cool, clinical years into which I have mistakenly been born, when everything has a reason until excuses pile up around even the most heinous story line. I need evil. No excuses.

I turn a stack of the heavy-hearted good books. Underneath there's an untidy row of battered paperbacks that quickens my pulse. The titles leap from the spines in blocky letters. I flick through them and find, in the second-last one, what I am and what I seek – the destiny proclaimed immediately by the cover. The title font is cold. Ominous, hand-rendered letters spell the words. Beneath them a woman, her bra torn from her shoulder, slumps beneath a streetlight. Like the lettering she is rendered by an intervening hand, the grimy concoction of an artist's leering gaze, a sordid studio and some anonymous girl – a grandmother now most likely – once in need of quick money. To the left foreground the artist has added the menace of a suited back and the squared fingers of the hand extending from it. Behind, a forest of fire-escapes above a line of dimly lit bars, their neons shimmering. But the image is all about her – her exposed pale skin, her hands rising in protest and protection, eyes wide. *Slave to Desire*.

I haggle over it out of habit. Regardless of price, it will be mine. The seller knows me too well. He keeps his premium but throws in another – *Angel Fears to Tread*, its cover torn but enticing.

As I pass you on my way home your glare towards me raises stifled laughs from the dwindling crowd. Your takings will be small. My advice, were you to ask – try something less esoteric. The cafés in the area are always on the lookout. You deserve no less than your No Fun Bird's attentions. I swing homeward, the books clasped tight beneath my coat as I hunch against a soft rain that has started falling. This place is supposed to be for romantic moments and strangers. I have mine. My night is made.

Bethany is waiting up. She keeps the hours of an owl. As soon as I show her my prize she squeals. Holds it to catch the light.

'What? I say.

'It's you, Em.'

And she's right. That dame on the cover (they're always dames). My eyes, my hair, my face. The same determinedly set jaw-line that gives me what Bethany calls my statue expression. The one I perfected for him. Almost impenetrable. Almost impossible to escape from. The one he mocked while I showered for him. Bastard.

You collect your bicycle from a lamppost and cycle home, your tragic face paint streaking, your heart heavier than your pockets. You wonder if it's worth it. You wish you could make random choices. But choices aren't like that. You know why you picked me. Of all the passing crowd, it was me you wanted. You thought you could have me, even for a moment. Even to humiliate. Dulled by apprehension, you cycle home through the rain to your dingy, one-room flat.

I cannot sleep. Tight nine-point type spells out a story's innocent beginnings. It shapes a worldly lecturer, a wide-eyed student taken in for private tutorials. The dark secrets she finds after her suspicions are aroused. The other woman. The others before her. The spectres and the lies.

Before I know it, I'm enmeshed. Because it is so familiar that it is me more than it is merely words on yellowing pages. And it's him too. Right down to the fishing trophies on his office wall, the unread books, the one prized review, predicting great things, framed on his mantel. And his strange obsessions.

Sickened by this new lust, I read into the morning. I am hauled onward by black stains on cockled white. The ink forms letters forming words. The words form a story I know even as it unfolds. The emptiness of never having completely cast hope aside. The wish to salvage something like love. The devotion of the jilted. *Slave to Desire.*

Next morning comes and goes. You stay in bed longer than you should, your thoughts awash with unformed despondency. Your costume, like your act, a bravura shroud designed to cover imperfection, lies crumpled on the chair beside your bed. You recall the glare of a stranger, a midnight girl who cursed you better than you cursed her. You cannot cast it off, as if an angry girl could haunt you more than all those dreams now playing out on cobblestones for loose change. The No Fun Bird hovers above you. Your own hex reflected and redoubled. The girl's face, so sharp it cut like a blade, stays with you – prevents you falling into the sleep you need. Tonight you must perform again.

I cycle through near-empty streets. Crews blast rubbish and vomit and accumulated dog-shit into the city's drains with hoses better suited for quelling riots. The shit makes its way under the churches and the galleries of art, under the palaces of the past, to the river. What a way to treat a city that thinks itself a woman.

In the basket that hangs from my handlebars *Slave to Desire* bumps along with the books I am supposed to have read, of Mallarmé and the symbolists. Monsieur Mallarmé has nothing I want. He was well enough treated in that other book. His book – *The Poets of Romance*. Better treated by its author than I ever was. But I choose the wrong one again. I choose the duplicitous pretender over the old master. I am returned to the lecturer by the paperback in the basket, and I know that before the day is over I will have sought him out. The humiliation of this seeking shall quiver inside me like the fuck of a boy I should never have invited to join me, who bangs me inexpertly as I try not to regurgitate a belly full of cheap wine. This shall be what I submit to – his grandfatherly eyes and the quickly hidden artefacts of his other lovers.

It is as I imagined. As I knew. Except that when I rap on his panelled oak door there is no reply. The whispering I hear from behind it could be imagined. The waft of a fruity perfume – the kind young girls think best suits their free spirits. All that is certain is that I am turned away – unfulfilled as if a door opening slowly, suspiciously, onto a university corridor would have changed everything. As if he would have longed for me, as I now do for him – with the desperation of an unfed dog for food.

In his absence I re-read the book that night. The story is all as I know it to be. Except that it ends where I have not yet taken it – where I know I must. It ends with Evangeline, who on the cover looks so much like me, fleeing back to the booksellers by the river. Which is where I find myself.

'So this is where my prettiest students spend their lonely evenings. Admirable. All these books. But sometimes …'

I know the rest of the line before he completes it. '… there are better places than this to spend the night.'

My next words come as if I am reading them from the yellowed pages. 'Better for you, perhaps. Ah, but there are things that I can show you, too. Things you have not yet even imagined…' And even though I know, now, how the rest of this story plays, I throw the book down and go with him. Half-running. Laughing in anticipation. Across the bridge and through the square. Past the vestiges of your last audience for the night.

You have barely covered the costs of the cigarettes and beer and chain-store hamburger you bought earlier in the day. Your rent is late again. You are packing up as he whisks me past – throwing your props and the hat you hold out like a beggar into an old sports bag, folding the drop-sheet that does for your stage.

You see the same look on my face but know that its meaning has changed. You know that between me and him it is different. He is so much older. You see only the things in him that I do not – his paunch, his mismatched socks, his intent so singular and lacking care it burns you. And so you sling the bag over your shoulder and follow. You are every bit as mad as I accused you of being the last time you tried to speak to me. You stay half a block behind almost to the Place de la Republique. You note the door into which we disappear, and then, a minute later, the light that turns on briefly in the front left window then turns out again.

There is always a twist. One ending that could be and another that is. It is not hard for you to scale the gate. Having climbed from it to the landing you pause to catch your breath and to listen for the sounds of us together. A window is unlocked. You are still wearing your costume. Your mask. He sees it as he turns at the sound of you pushing through his bedroom door.

Rodeo

W e'd had years on the circuit, playing rodeos and country shows, town halls and festivals. Years of fighting and splitting and getting back together. Always the song. I told him he could sing anything else to anyone else but that song was just for me. It had been a big hit when he needed one. It saved him in many ways, and it still got the biggest response from fans. Even tonight it sounded as good as when I first heard him sing it. Because when he sings it you hold your breath.

The record company had called me in. That song you sent us. We want Clem to have it. Sure, I said. Then they shoved a paper in front of me and next thing he's got it alright. By the time the record came out – words and music: Clem Mullins – we were together and that song was never going to let us be apart for long.

Now I'm alone while a sweet country girl with fame in her eyes shares a bottle with him. I drop the needle on the crackling track.

The long haul

The first thing he saw was the dust cloud beside the distant line of river gums. Dean put the kettle on. By the time Hattie eased down through ten gears and rumbled to a stop he had her coffee made the way she liked it, milky instant with three sugars.

'Good run?'

Hattie jumped down. 'Easy. Bit of rain outside Dubbo.'

'They fixed up the road yet?' He'd driven that same pot-holed two-lane a thousand times before his back went.

The injury could have been the end for them. Everything they had was in that truck. That's when Hattie said, 'Teach me.'

'You mean it? It's no picnic.'

'You want us to chuck it all in instead? Nah, I reckon I'm up for it.'

Now she was known in every roadhouse on the East Coast and the loan on the rig had been paid. Hattie acquired a cowboy hat and her own line in truck-stop small talk along with the girth of a long-distance driver. She rolled across the continent while Dean waited, the way she'd once done for him.

With the sun setting across the dam Dean and Hattie settled into yarning.

'Like a couple of old sheilas,' said Dean, chuckling. Crickets struck up nearby. Stars flecked the darkening sky.

ACKNOWLEDGEMENTS Like crafting flash, I'll try to keep this short. Thanks first to my wonderful writing colleagues for their good counsel through the years, and for remaining always able to tell me when things weren't working. Special thanks to the current unruly crew: Ilka, Suzy, Brooke, Carla, Melinda and Michelle.

Thanks, Oliver, for patience and diligence and for treating my manuscript with the care I hope it deserved. Thanks, Bettina, for taking ideas that were only ever words and reinventing them as magical marks that dance alongside.

To Bronwyn, the heart and soul of the very wonderful (and decidedly not spineless) Spineless Wonders, many, many thanks.

And thanks forever to Thomas and Polly, because there's no story worth telling without the two of you.

Richard Holt

NOTES Some stories in this book have been published elsewhere, as follows:

'Afloat', *Out of Place*, Spineless Wonders, 2015
'Fading towards infinity', *Victorian Writer Fiction Edition*, Writers Victoria, 2015
'The working man's struggle', *Eating my Words*, Gumbo Press, 2014
'The swimmer', *Stoned Crows & other Australian icons*, Spineless Wonders, 2013.
'Her dark ground', *Writing to the Edge*, Spineless Wonders, 2014
'Free market', *Flashing the Square*, Spineless Wonders, 2014
'Oblong', *Landmarks*, Spineless Wonders, 2016
'The gambler', *Landmarks*, Gumbo Press, 2015
'… but it falls', *Visible Ink #23*, RMIT, 2011
'Particle physics', *Flashing the Square*, Spineless Wonders, 2014
'Bush burial', *Stoned Crows & other Australian Icons*, Spineless Wonders, 2013

SPINELESS WONDERS
short Australian stories – *everywhere*

www.shortaustralianstories.com.au